Clambakes and Chaos
A Nanny Blu Cozy Mystery

Summer in Diamond Bay
Book 5

By

Maci Grant

TABLE OF CONTENTS

CHAPTER 1

It would usually take an act of God to convince Blu to wake up the kids earlier than normal. The last thing she wanted was a cranky four-year-old and a moody seven-year-old on her hands. Today, however, she knew that they'd be even more upset if they woke up to discover that they'd missed their chance to dig for clams.

It was the end-of-summer celebration for all the summer visitors that stayed in the beach houses as well as the local residents of Diamond Bay. The community event had been advertised for the past few weeks all over town. There was no way for the kids not to hear about the early morning clam dig, and they were very excited to be part of it.

"Let's go, Joey, we have to dig some clams today." Blu gave his shoulder a little shake.

Joey sprang right out of bed. "Yes, I can't wait!"

"Well, you're going to have to wait. We need to have breakfast first, okay?"

"Aw!"

"It's important to have a full belly if you want to work hard." Blu ruffled his hair. "Get dressed. Make sure you wear sneakers, okay?"

"Okay." He headed for his closet.

Blu left his room to wake up Marley next.

"Morning, sweetheart, we're going to get up now." She tickled one of Marley's palms.

"No." Marley whined and scooted away from her across the bed.

"Marley, we have to get up if we want to go dig for clams."

"Clams?" Marley sat up. "Yes! I'm up!"

"Good girl." Blu laughed. "Let's find something for you to wear."

Blu made sure both kids were dressed in something acceptable for the activity, then she gave them a quick breakfast of cereal and fruit. Just as they finished, there was a knock on the kitchen door.

Blu looked through the glass to see that it was AJ. She smiled and crossed the room to open the door.

"Are we ready to dig for some clams?" AJ smiled at the kids.

"Yes!" Both children shouted, jumping up and charging straight for AJ.

"Brace yourself!" Blu laughed.

AJ grabbed on to the doorway to keep from getting knocked over as the two kids tried to tackle him with hugs. AJ's eyes lit up as he looked past them to Blu. Blu held his gaze as a warm smile spread across her lips, but it faded just a little as she was reminded of what the clambake meant.

It meant that summer was coming to an end. Whatever could have happened between her and AJ was never going to happen, which meant that soon they'd be forced to say goodbye. Her heart ached a little more than she expected it to.

"Are you guys ready to go? Do I even really need to ask?"

"Just let me grab my purse," said Blu.

"Okay, we'll meet you at the jeep."

"Will you grab the chairs out of the trunk of my car?" Blu tossed him the keys.

AJ caught them in midair. For a split second their eyes met. Blu had an odd sensation of being flung forward into a time when the two excited kids between them didn't belong to someone else.

The thought startled her.

AJ turned and escorted the kids outside.

Blu's heart fluttered. How could she begin picturing him as the potential future father of her children when they hadn't even been on an official date? It was foolish.

"In two days I will be a memory to him. That's it." Blu grabbed her purse and did her best to keep her heart under control.

When she joined AJ and the kids at his jeep she

double-checked their seat belts. Blu took her job as a nanny very seriously, especially when it came to the safety of the children she cared for.

When she settled into the front seat beside AJ, he started the car and backed out of the driveway. Despite how comfortable she'd become around him over the past months, after the flash-forward she'd just had, the awkwardness returned.

"So, are you guys excited to dig up some clams?" AJ glanced in the rearview mirror at the kids.

"I'm going to get one hundred!" Marley clapped.

"Marley." Joey sighed. "There's no way that you're going to get one hundred clams. We've talked about numbers, remember?"

"It's okay, Joey. It's important to believe in things, even if they seem impossible." AJ glanced over at Blu.

She looked back at him with a slight smile. It was sweet of him to support Marley, but she wondered if there might be an underlying message in his words. AJ certainly hadn't been shy about his desire to explore a romantic relationship with her. But Blu was determined not to start any relationships that wouldn't be headed somewhere. She was ready for something long-term, not just a little summer fling.

"The important thing is to keep an open mind and just give it a shot," AJ continued.

With that comment, Blu smirked as she looked out the window. His attempt to bait her was obvious and she remained determined not to respond to it.

"Today we dig for clams, tomorrow we dine. Right, kids?" said Blu.

"Yes." Joey rocked back and forth in his seat. "When are we going to get there?"

"Here we are." AJ eased the jeep into the beach parking lot. There were several other cars parked along the sand.

Blu unloaded the kids and the four walked up to a small white tent.

"Get your shovels, get your buckets!" The man behind the table smiled at the four. "Welcome."

"Thanks." Blu took one of the shovels and handed it to Joey. "Here you go. Now you're officially a clammer, Joey."

"Alright!"

"I think a smaller one will work for the little lady." He handed Marley a small plastic shovel.

Marley's nose crinkled up, but she took the shovel with a reluctant nod.

"And for Mom and Dad?" The man grinned.

"Uh—not Mom and Dad." Blu stumbled over her words.

"She's our nanny." Joey giggled.

"Oops, my mistake. Shovels?"

Blu and AJ each took one from the man.

They walked toward the mud just as Blu's best friend, Maddie, walked up to them.

CHAPTER 2

Blu grinned at her friend. "Maddie! I'm so glad you're here!"

Maddie lifted her dark sunglasses to peer at Blu. "Trust me, I'm not."

"Too early?" AJ grinned.

"Far, far too early." Maddie shook her head. "I should be hitting the snooze button right now."

"Isn't this so much better?" Blu looked out over the water, which glowed gold in the early morning sunlight. "It's gorgeous out."

"True. I guess we should be appreciating it since we only have a few days left here."

"Good point." Blu smiled at Chrissa and Brennan, the two kids that Maddie looked after. "Morning."

"Morning." Brennan waved to her then took off across the mud. Chrissa spotted some friends and took off as well.

"It seems a bit more like social hour than a time for digging." Maddie yawned. "So what's the deal with all this? Do we all have to dig?"

"No. It's just for fun. The clammers get most of the clams for the clambake. But it's nice to participate, and I thought it would be a good experience for the kids."

"Joey seems to like it." AJ tilted his head toward the young boy, who already had a shovel and was poking at the mud.

"Oh boy, I think Marley likes it even more." Blu ran over to Marley, who was elbows deep in the mud.

AJ and Maddie laughed as Blu tugged the girl's hands loose.

"Okay, on that note, I'll be on the beach." Maddie turned and walked off across the sand with her phone in her hand.

AJ crouched down in front of Marley.

"Why don't we get you a shovel, hm?"

"I like to dig." Marley giggled and shoved her hands right back down in the mud.

AJ turned toward Blu. "So what are you going to do when you get back to the big city?"

Blu watched Marley fling a clump of mud with her shovel. "Probably more of the same, only with lots more traffic." She winked.

"Nice." AJ looked out over the water. "Do you get days off in the city too?"

"Yes."

"Weekends?"

"Sometimes."

"That's good." AJ kicked the toe of his boot down

into a pile of mud. "Do you think you might want to show me around the city?"

Blu cleared her throat. "Marley, please don't put the mud in your hair."

Marley brought her hands down from her head and blinked innocently.

Blu pretended that she hadn't heard AJ's question. Eventually she would have to tell him the truth—that things couldn't go any farther—but she didn't want to ruin their last days together. Maybe it was a bit selfish of her, but she wanted to enjoy every moment that she had with AJ before she had to let him go.

"You do realize that you still owe me a dinner?" He paused just beside her.

Blu had no way to claim that she didn't hear what he said.

"I'm aware."

"And?" His elbow brushed lightly against hers.

"And how about tomorrow?"

"You mean the clambake?"

"Yes. We could both attend."

"Together?" AJ quirked a brow. "Like a date?"

"Like a clambake." Blu laughed and chased Marley across the mud.

When she looked back, AJ stood in the same spot with his hands shoved into the pockets of his jeans. He squinted at her through the morning sun in a way that made his features come alive with character. She sighed as she studied him.

A part of her regretted spending the entire summer talking herself out of anything with AJ. It could have been fun if she'd just let it happen. Instead, she was faced with missing out on a chemistry that she couldn't deny no matter how hard she tried.

Blu helped Marley dig up a couple of clams. AJ held the bucket out for them. Every brush and accidental touch distracted Blu. Each one sent a spiral of warmth through her, followed by the cold reality that it would all end soon.

She glanced around the beach, suddenly aware that she couldn't see Joey anywhere.

"Where's Joey?" Blu searched more intently.

It had been several minutes since she'd last laid eyes on him. Normally she kept the children in sight at all times, but Joey had been known to wander off. Just as she started to feel a flutter of panic rise up through her chest, she saw him.

He ran toward them with a strange tool in his hand. It looked a bit like a bent rake.

"What's that, Joey?" Blu asked.

"Hey, buddy, be careful with that." AJ walked up to him. "Where did you get this?" He took the wooden handle of the tool.

"It was just lying on the beach. Isn't it cool?" Joey grinned.

"It is cool. It's a clam hoe. Clammers use them to dig

out the clams. It's a little strange that a clammer would leave it lying on the beach, though. Are you sure there was no one around?"

"No." Joey frowned. "I wouldn't have taken it if I thought it belonged to someone, honest."

"Well, whoever left it there was pretty foolish." AJ's jaw clenched. He looked up at Blu. "These tines can be sharp. This beach is full of kids. Whoever did this should know better."

"Maybe we should take it up to the tent?" Blu looked over at the tent set up near the parking lot.

"No, first I want to make sure it doesn't belong to someone. Joey, can you show me where you found it?"

"Sure." Joey nodded.

Blu grabbed Marley's muddy hand.

AJ walked beside Joey with the clam hoe in hand, Blu and Marley following after them.

"Slurp, slurp, slurp." Marley giggled as her shoes sank into the mud.

"It was right there." Joey pointed to a spot in the mud beside an overturned rowboat.

"What's that boat doing there? That's weird, isn't it?" Blu narrowed her eyes. "Won't it be swept away when the tide comes in?"

"Yes, it will be. It is odd." AJ walked toward the boat. "It looks like someone left their hip waders behind too." He gestured to the high boots that stuck out from beneath the edge of the boat. "We can take it all up to the tent."

Blu nodded.

AJ reached down and grabbed the foot of one of the boots. When he did, Blu recognized something instantly change with his body language. She tried to catch his eye to see what was wrong. His expression was strained as he straightened back up.

"Let's just take the clam hoe. Joey, Marley, let's go together, okay?"

He guided the kids back up along the sand.

Blu could tell that something was very wrong.

CHAPTER 3

Blu was too curious not to see what the problem was for herself. She walked over to the rowboat and grabbed one of the boots. Right away she could tell that there was actually a foot inside the boot. She dropped it and ducked down to look under the boat.

Underneath was a man—face down in the mud. She gave his leg a hard shake to see if maybe he was somehow asleep. When she did she could tell that he was stiff.

She stumbled back as the reality of what they'd just discovered hit her.

"Blu!" AJ frowned as he looked over at her. "Let's go. We need to get the kids away from here." He already had his phone in his hand. "I'm calling my uncle."

Blu nodded, too dazed to speak. Her attention lingered on the mud beside the boat, which was rutted as if the body had been pulled across it.

"Blu." AJ's voice was quiet.

Her eyes shifted to the three who were already up on

the sand. She snapped back to reality when she saw the concern on Joey's face. Her shoes stuck in the mud as she trudged toward them.

"Did I do something wrong, Blu? Why is AJ calling Chief Pitman? I didn't steal it, honest."

"I know you didn't, Joey. You didn't do anything wrong." She put her arm around his shoulders. "It's just fine, okay? We have some clams to dig up, don't we?"

"Yes." He smiled.

Blu led the kids away from AJ so that he could speak freely on the phone to his uncle. They rejoined the rest of the group in the main area of the clam dig.

Maddie stood in the sand with her arms folded as she watched Chrissa and Brennan, who were just standing off to the side a bit. "They wanted to come but they haven't dug up a single clam." Maddie shook her head. "I don't think I'm ever going to figure out teenagers."

"Trust me, it's not worth trying." Blu frowned. "There's a problem."

"What is it?"

Blu leaned close and whispered to Maddie what they'd found. As if to punctuate her words, a patrol car with lights flashing pulled into the parking lot.

"Ugh." Maddie looked from the parking lot to the crowd of people spread out across the mud. "Do you think they'll clear us out?"

"I doubt it. It's a way down the beach, so they should be able to investigate without us having to leave. I don't think Joey has any idea what he found."

"Well. that's one good thing." Maddie pulled out her phone and tapped the screen. "Nothing about it on the web yet. So you're likely the only ones that know. I don't know about you but I'm looking forward to getting back to Manhattan."

"I am, but—" Blu cleared her throat.

"—But AJ?" Maddie glanced over at Blu just as AJ walked toward them.

"There's that." Blu forced a smile.

"Hon, it's only like an hour away. I say, if you want it, go for it."

Blu nodded, but she knew that it was about more than just the physical distance. It was an entirely different life. Maybe AJ would want to drive there a few times, maybe she'd meet him at the beach now and then, but in the long run, the chance of anything really working out between them seemed impossible to her.

"Hey." AJ glanced between the two. "Are the kids okay?"

"I don't think they have any idea what happened." Blu peered at him as she shaded her eyes with one hand. "Did you find anything out?"

"Yes. The man under the boat is George Hunt. He's a local clammer and fisherman. He lives on his boat."

"What a shame." Blu frowned.

Maddie shook her head. "I don't know how many

people will agree with you. George is known as a bit of a troublemaker around here. He's often drunk and combative with residents."

"No shortage of enemies then, hm?"

AJ lifted his shoulders in a mild shrug. "It's hard to say. It's clear that he was killed, though we can't say how just yet."

"What a way to end the summer," Maddie said. "It probably won't bode well for the clambake."

"Oh, trust me, the show will go on." AJ shook his head as he continued. "This event is sponsored every year by a local councilman, James Carry. He's very anti-drug, and every event he puts on is centered around drug abuse prevention. He won't let this stop him from hosting the clambake. In fact, I doubt he'd let a hurricane stop him. He's a very determined man."

"Well, that's good, I guess. I'd hate for the kids to miss out on the clambake. If this man was as shady as you say he was, then he probably got mixed up with the wrong person and ended up under that boat," said Blu.

"It's very likely." AJ nodded. "It looks like they're about done with the dig. How about if I take you and the kids home to change and then we have lunch?"

"Oh, I don't know." Blu bit into her bottom lip.

Maddie shoved her with her elbow. "She'd love to. Right, Blu?"

"Yes. Yes, I would." Blu managed a smile.

AJ grinned at Maddie. Then he waved the kids in

from the mud.

They turned in their clams and shovels and then headed for the parking lot.

"Maddie, do you and the kids want to join us?" Blu looked at her friend, hoping that she'd accept the invitation.

"Not this time. I have to get the kids to a party for their boating class. We should be back by three if you want to stop by."

"Thanks." Blu smiled at Chrissa and Brennan. "Have fun at your party."

"Thanks." The kids said their goodbyes. Blu wiped Marley down as well as she could, then helped her into her seat.

Joey gazed toward the water. "Blu, what are all the police cars doing at the beach?"

Blu looked in the same direction and saw a semicircle of patrol cars gathered near the rowboat.

"They're just looking into something Joey—nothing to worry about."

Joey nodded, but Blu noticed that his frown didn't fade until they drove away from the beach.

Blu wondered if Joey had picked up more than she'd realized about the situation.

CHAPTER 4

When they arrived at the house, Blu paused at the door with AJ. "You know, maybe we should skip lunch. Joey seems a little upset."

"All the more reason to go out, don't you think?" AJ met her eyes. "If we keep him distracted, I'm sure he'll forget all about what he saw this morning. Besides, I don't think he saw much."

"I guess." Blu frowned. "I just hate to see him look so worried."

"I can have my uncle talk to him if he's still upset tonight."

"Good idea." Blu nodded. "We'll just be a minute— help yourself to anything in the kitchen."

She escorted Marley to the bathroom to wash up while Joey changed in his room. As Blu scrubbed the mud out from under Marley's fingernails, the little girl looked up at her with wide eyes.

"Are you sad, Blu?"

"Hm?" Blu looked into her eyes. "Why do you think that?"

"You look sad."

"How's this?" Blu smiled.

"No. It's your eyes." Marley sighed and shook her head. "Smiles don't fix that."

Blu quirked an eyebrow at the child's wise words. "Well, today something sad happened, so maybe I'm a little sad. But it's nothing to worry about, okay?"

"I thought you were sad because of AJ."

"Why would AJ make me sad?"

"I don't know. Want me to kick him?"

Blu did her best not to laugh. "Marley, it's not nice to kick people."

"Even if they make you sad?"

"Even if they make you sad. But AJ doesn't make me sad. He's a very nice man, and he makes me very happy."

"Oh." Marley shrugged. "Grown-ups are weird."

"That's because we're not allowed to kick people." Blu sighed.

Marley giggled.

"Ready to go eat?"

"Yes! I'm starving!" Marley raced into the hallway and nearly knocked into AJ, who had just stepped out of Joey's room.

He met Blu's eyes with a light smile. "Joey was showing me his collection of superheroes."

"Oh, it's great, isn't it?" Blu felt her cheeks warm. Had he heard what she'd said to Marley?

"Yes, it is. Ready to go?"

"Absolutely." Blu guided the kids back to the jeep.

AJ drove them to the beach.

"The cafe has a special right now because of the clambake. I thought the kids would like it. They'll get a bucket filled with stickers, coloring pages, and crayons."

"Do you think everything's cleared up?" asked Blu.

"I'm sure it is." AJ nodded. "My uncle texted me that things were tidied up. It doesn't surprise me. James Carry probably lit a fire under someone to make sure the situation wouldn't interfere with the clambake."

AJ parked the jeep in front of the beachside cafe. Blu had eaten there many times throughout the summer. It was one of the kids' favorite spots because in the outside seating area, the seagulls would try to steal hot dog buns and other treats right off their plates.

"Maybe we should eat inside, just in case?"

"Sure." AJ opened the door for all three of them.

They sat down at a table that faced the road instead of the beach. Once they'd placed their order, AJ looked across the table at Blu. "So about what we were discussing earlier."

"What was that?" Blu picked up her glass of water and took a sip.

"About your weekends off." He leaned across the table, and Blu didn't miss the fact that he was attempting to lock his eyes with hers. She was pretty sure that AJ wanted more than just their typical lighthearted conversation.

Blu suddenly found everything around her very interesting. Her eyes wandered in every direction but AJ's.

"Blu?"

"You're AJ, aren't you?"

The strange voice startled both of them out of their visual dance. A waitress stood beside the table. She fluttered her hands at her sides and glanced around before looking back at AJ.

"Chief Pitman's nephew?"

"Yes." AJ studied her. "Do we know each other?"

"Just from around. I mean, I know you're related to the chief."

"Yes, that's true. Is there something I can help you with?"

"It's more like something I can help him with." She looked around again, then lowered her voice. "I open the restaurant every morning. Once a week, every week, George Hunt is down by the mud, just like he was this morning."

"Oh? Did you see what happened?" AJ shifted in his chair to look directly at the waitress.

"I don't want my name in any of this, understand? I wouldn't be saying anything at all, but I just don't think it's right. George didn't deserve to die like that."

Blu looked at her nametag. "Cathy, you don't have to worry. You can tell us anything. What did you see?"

"It's what I didn't see. Usually this other guy meets up

with George. You know—for a deal." She quirked an eyebrow.

"Oh?" AJ cleared his throat. "So, what happened this morning?"

"Well, I saw George down there. As I was getting the cafe ready to open, I looked out the window and I saw the guy he always meets. But George wasn't there. And when I saw the other guy, he took off real fast."

"Do you know who this other guy is?" AJ held her gaze.

"I can't say." She fiddled with her order pad.

"Because you never met him?" Blu prompted.

"I just can't say."

"If you know his name, I need to know." AJ tapped his phone. "I can let my uncle know right now."

"No, I can't. I told you I don't want to be involved in any of this. If any cops come here and ask me questions, I won't tell them anything. The only reason I'm telling you is because I know that you'll tell your uncle. I feel bad for George and that this happened here, but I can't tell you the name of the guy. I think he's dangerous and involved with even more dangerous people."

"You have to tell me." AJ reached for her hand, but Blu caught it before he could make contact.

"Wait, Cathy. I understand why you're scared. No one is going to make you do anything you don't want to do." She held on to AJ's hand, which tensed in her grasp. "But maybe you could help us by giving us an idea of what he

29

looked like—maybe what kind of car he drove? No one will know that it was you who gave us that information, okay?"

CHAPTER 5

Cathy looked at AJ with her lips drawn into a tight line, then nodded. "Okay. He's in his early twenties. He has black hair—kinda shaggy, but not past his neck. He's tall with some muscles."

"That's all good." AJ nodded. "And the car?"

"It's a motorcycle—the kind with a big compartment in the back. It's where he puts the—well, you know."

"What?" AJ raised an eyebrow.

Cathy looked at the kids, who were busy coloring their pictures. She whispered. "Drugs."

"George was involved in that?"

"Yes. I mean, I don't know for sure. Like I said, I'll deny it if anyone asks. But I just want all of this to be over, and I don't want that guy to come back."

"You've helped us a lot, Cathy."

"Remember what I said." She locked eyes with AJ. "I don't want my name in any of this."

"It won't be." Blu smiled at her. "It's going to be fine. Try not to worry."

As the waitress walked away from the table, AJ looked at Blu with his brows knitted. "Why did you tell her that?"

"Tell her what?"

"That we would keep her name out of this?"

"Because we will. She asked us to, so we will." Blu tilted her head to the side. "You're not going to tell your uncle her name, are you?"

"Of course I am. It's important information." AJ narrowed his eyes. "He can protect her."

"AJ, if someone gives you information, it's like a sacred pact. You can't just reveal a source."

"I'm a bar owner, not a reporter." He shook his head. "I know my uncle. He's going to want to know a name."

"Then you just tell him that I told you, and I won't reveal who gave me the information."

"You would do that? Tempt my uncle's temper?"

"Sure." Blu looked over at Cathy, whose hand shook as she refilled coffee cups. "That woman is terrified. I made her a promise. I intend to keep it."

"You're a very brave woman, Blu."

"I just try to do what I think is right. Sometimes it's not about what's easy, it's about what's right."

He studied her for a moment, then nodded. Their original waitress brought over their food.

Blu began to eat, but her mind was elsewhere. How had she been in the beach town all summer and not known that such dangerous things were taking place? It left her feeling more than a little unsettled.

"Alright, I won't tell him her name." AJ looked across the table at her. "But I can't promise you that my uncle won't be determined to find out."

"If the information pans out, then maybe he'll be too distracted to hunt her down."

"Maybe."

When they'd finished their food AJ drove them back to the beach house. He lingered by the door once the kids were inside.

"I'm going to go talk to my uncle. I'll let you know if anything new comes up."

"Okay." Blu smiled.

"Blu, I still want to talk about things."

She lowered her eyes. "I'm not sure what." She was surprised when she felt his palm curve beneath her chin.

He tilted her head upward with a gentle pressure. "Yes, you are." He searched her eyes as his fingertips stroked along the curve of her chin. "You're as sure as I am. That's why we need to talk."

"Later." Blu barely managed to get the word out. The way AJ was looking at her caused her knees to weaken. Her head spun with the force of what her instincts demanded.

"Later." He nodded and gave her chin a light tap. Then he turned and walked back to his jeep.

Blu leaned against the doorway to keep herself upright.

"Oh, Blu, what have you gotten yourself into?" She shook her head and stepped into the house.

When she closed the door behind her, she hoped to close out some of the wild sensations that coursed through her, but no amount of wood or glass could eliminate the connection she'd already experienced with AJ.

In an attempt to distract herself from what she was feeling, Blu turned on the television as she and the kids walked into the living room. She'd planned to turn on some cartoons to help the kids relax a bit after such an adventurous day, but it was the local news channel that grabbed her attention. Before she could turn it, the reporter on the screen began to describe the beach scene that was already foremost on Blu's mind.

"In the kitchen, kids." Blu shooed them toward the kitchen. Her gaze remained on the screen as the reporter described the victim.

"In an apparent drug deal gone wrong, a man is dead today. He was found on the beach this morning during the annual end of the summer clam dig. Luckily, the body was located far enough away from the crowd that it didn't interfere with the festivities. Let's listen to a few comments that Councilman James Carry shared about the situation earlier this morning."

"Once more our peaceful town is tarnished by the blight of drug trafficking. I can't say enough about how disappointed I am at the timing of this event. At the very least, there's one less drug dealer in this town. I can assure you that whoever committed this crime will be caught and penalized for it. In the meantime, the clambake must go on. We can't allow the influence of something as toxic and cruel as drugs stop us from having a successful end-of-the-summer celebration. We cannot—no, we will not—allow these people to ruin our paradise."

CHAPTER 6

Blu turned off the television as the camera cut away from the councilman. It made her a little uncomfortable to think that a man's life could be less important than a clambake, even if he was a drug dealer—and as far as she was concerned, that was still an if.

"Let's do some art, kids. Sound good?" Blu wanted to keep their minds off what had happened that morning.

"Paints!" Marley grinned.

"Oh, yes, paints—messy, messy paints." Blu laughed. "Better than mud, right?"

"Maybe."

"I don't want to do art." Joey sighed. "Art is for babies."

"Let's see if you can draw me something that has to do with the clambake, hm?" She smiled at him. "Maybe something you saw or did this morning that you enjoyed?"

"Do I have to?" He looked up at her with wide eyes and lips curled in a pout.

"Just this once. For me?" Blu handed him a piece of

white drawing paper.

Joey sighed and took it from her.

"Take it to the kitchen table, please."

Joey moped his way to the kitchen table with the paper.

Blu and Marley gathered the paints and more paper. Blu filled some small containers with water for the kids to dip their paintbrushes in. She watched as the kids settled into their art activity. She did try to encourage them to be creative, but she had another motive behind the assignment. She was curious whether Joey had seen more than what he'd said. She thought that he might feel more comfortable communicating it in a picture.

While the kids painted at the kitchen table, Blu cleaned up the kitchen. She decided to give Maddie a call and update her on the latest information.

"So you think it's all drug related?" Maddie asked. "Nowhere is safe any more, is it?"

"Nowhere that money can be made from illegal activity, that's for sure."

Blu glanced over at the kids' paintings. So far, Marley's featured a big pile of mud and Joey's looked as if he was attempting to draw every individual piece of sand. Her attention turned back to Maddie on the other end of the phone line. "But at least we know the name of the victim, and Chief Pitman should be able to get an ID of the man who was meeting with him from the description the waitress gave us."

"I wonder why she's so afraid of having her name involved?"

"Who knows? Maybe she's been threatened by him before. If they've been meeting at the beach regularly she might have had a run-in with them."

"That's true. I don't blame her for being careful. Sometimes it seems like the police can't do much to protect people."

"I agree. That's why I think it might be a good idea to look into this ourselves."

"Really? Why?"

"I just think that it can't hurt to have another set of investigators on the crime. Right?"

"You and your journalistic nature. You just can't leave it alone, can you?" Maddie's voice grew lighter with amusement.

"It just bugs me a little. Everyone is so quick to call this man scum, but he was still a man. I wonder if there isn't something more to him. I just feel like I'd like to know more about who he was."

"Would you like me to look into him?"

"Yes, I would. If you want to." She sweetened her voice.

"Sure. I'll find out what I can. But I hope you won't be disappointed. Sometimes what you see really is all you get."

"I know, I know. But I guess there's a part of me that believes there's always some kind of redeeming quality to a person."

"I believe that you are one of the softies."

"I'm not a softie!"

"Sure, if you say so. I'll let you know what I find."

"Great. Thanks, Maddie." Blu hung up the phone and turned back to the kids. When she looked at their paintings she smiled. "Amazing artists in this house. Marley, is that me that you're throwing mud at?"

"Yup." Marley swung her feet under the table and giggled.

"And Joey, I love how specific your drawing is. I see the rowboat that we saw this morning."

"Yup. And the clam hoe." He pointed out the tool in the sand beside the rowboat.

Blu was relieved to see that he did not draw the hip waders sticking out from under the boat. She assumed he hadn't put two and two together about the news report and what he'd painted. She did notice, however, something strange in the sand not far from the boat that he'd painted.

"What's that, Joey?" She pointed to a bright yellow circle in the sand.

"Oh, it's a ring. I saw it in the sand this morning."

"Hm—you didn't mention that earlier today." Blu raised an eyebrow.

"I forgot. I knew it wasn't mine, and I thought someone might come back for it, so I left it there. It wasn't until I started drawing the sand that I remembered.

It was shiny—that's why I noticed it. But the clam hoe was way cooler."

"Did it have a stone of some kind in it? Like a diamond or a ruby?"

"No, but I think it had some letters on it."

"Do you remember what they were?" Blu leaned closer to him.

Joey tucked his lower lip under his teeth and looked up at the ceiling. Then he painted two letters onto his picture.

"A and L? Those are the letters that you saw?"

"Yes." Joey smiled. "I think so. It's hard to remember."

"Thanks for telling me." She smiled. "Your painting is wonderful."

"Thank you. But it's not done yet." He went back to his painting.

CHAPTER 7

Blu wondered if the ring Joey had painted might lead them to some evidence. Had the killer left it behind? Did George leave it there? She picked up her phone to call AJ, but when she looked down his name was already on her screen, indicating an incoming call.

"Hello?" Blu smiled. "I was just about to call you."

"Aha, great minds think alike."

"I guess so." Blu tried to ignore the flutter of her heart.

"I wanted to give you an update on the case. My uncle let me know that George died as a result of being held down in the mud."

"Oh, how awful."

"Yes, it is." He cleared his throat. "He might not have been a good man, but no one deserves to die like that."

"Did you tell the chief about the man that Cathy saw?"

"Yes. Boy, did that conversation not go well. He let me know that he wasn't happy I wouldn't tell him who saw the man. Don't be surprised if he calls to question you."

"I won't be." Blu rolled her eyes. "I have something to tell you too. If you want to pass it on to your uncle it's okay, but I'd rather Joey not be involved."

"I understand. What is it?"

"I had the kids paint pictures of their fun this morning, and Joey painted the rowboat."

"But he didn't see what was underneath, did he?"

"I don't think so. But he did paint a gold ring in the sand. He said it was there when he found the clam hoe. I thought it might be of use to the case."

"Hm. I'll check with my uncle to see if it was logged into evidence."

"Great."

"Blu, can we get some time alone tonight—to talk?"

"Oh, I don't know. I think Rachel is going to need me to watch the kids tonight."

AJ was silent on the other end of the phone. The silence said a lot more than any words could. When he finally spoke his voice was rougher than usual.

"Then we'll see each other tomorrow at the clambake?"

"Absolutely."

Blu hung up the phone before he could say anything else. Her heart pounded as she gripped the phone. She knew that time was running out. She was going to have to be willing to talk to AJ eventually. The only problem was, she wasn't at all sure what she'd have to say. Was she going to tell him that it was over between them before anything had really begun? Or was she going to offer the opportunity for them to get together later after she'd left the beach? It was hard for her to figure out what she wanted, so how could she possibly expect him to understand her confusion?

"Alright, kids, let's clean up. Your mom should be home soon."

Blu took their paintings and put them on the back porch to dry. As she looked out at the water she felt a subtle tug. She would miss the beach life when they returned to the city, but if she was honest with herself, it wasn't so much the sun and the sand that had her heart, but the man whom she was doing her very best to avoid.

When Blu stepped back inside, her cell phone was ringing. She picked it up to see that it was Maddie. "Hello?"

"Hi, Blu. I thought you might want to know what I found out about George."

"Yes, that would be great."

"I am getting to know George very well, thanks to his ex-wife Betty. She's been blasting him all over social media. Apparently she's remarried, but the marriage isn't considered legal because George never followed through with his end of the paperwork. I don't even think she knows that George is dead yet. Her latest post is about him not showing up for a meeting this morning."

"Interesting. I wonder if the police have spoken to her?"

"They might not, since technically they aren't married."

"Do you have her address?"

"Yes, it's only about twenty minutes away. Do you want me to watch the kids so that you can go talk to her?"

"Oh, you know me far too well."

"Yes. Yes, I do."

"I'll be there in ten minutes."

"Ha, more like seven."

"Now you're pushing it."

"We'll see." Maddie laughed as they hung up the phone.

Blu herded the kids into the car. Both were quite excited to go see Brennan and Chrissa.

When Blu pulled into the driveway it had been exactly seven minutes. She sat in the car until it was eight, then she and the kids walked up to the front door. Blu knocked and Maddie swung the door open with a big smile on her face.

"Detective Blu, I presume?"

"Indeed."

"I saw you sitting in the driveway." Maddie shook her head. "It was seven minutes."

"Maybe you're the detective." Blu laughed.

"I like to think of myself as your research assistant. You know, the perky sidekick that does all of the actual work."

"Perky, yes." Blu ducked as Maddie swung a playful punch at her.

"So I suppose these little rugrats are mine now, hm?" Maddie winked at Marley and Joey.

"Just for a little while." Blu grinned.

"It's no problem. Chrissa has been dying to get her hands on Marley's hair again. This time I promise, no hair dye."

"Good." Blu laughed.

"Is Brennan home?" Joey slid past Blu and Maddie into the house.

"He's upstairs playing a new video game, Joey."

"Yes!" Joey raced up the stairs.

"Looks like they're going to have a fun afternoon. Thanks, Maddie."

"Just remember this when I'm calling you for help figuring out Brennan's math homework." She shook her head. "Never in my life did I think I'd be doing homework again."

CHAPTER 8

Blu walked back to her car with a smile on her lips. She enjoyed being able to share the trials of being a nanny with Maddie. Sure, it was a fun job, but it wasn't always easy.

As she drove toward the address that she'd programmed into her GPS, she wondered what she'd find when she arrived. Maddie had forwarded her a few of Betty's posts, and they weren't very nice at all. The woman used colorful language to depict exactly what she'd do to her ex-husband when she saw him again.

There was no question of motive there, but Blu knew of plenty of ex-spouses that had motive to kill. That didn't make them all murderers.

It wasn't long before Blu turned down a sparsely inhabited street. The properties were large, but Betty's home was the smallest of the bunch. The home was a sprawling ranch with several cars parked out front.

Blu parked between two of the cars. She took the time to study the environment for a few minutes, as she had no idea what she was walking into. Right away she noticed large boots outside the front door. There was also a pair of shears propped up against the side of the porch. The yard was neat, but not flourishing. It was just a simple home.

She opened her car door and stepped out. When she walked up the driveway, she saw that the garage door needed a fresh coat of paint. The gutters along the front of the house sagged.

She knocked on the front door and waited for an answer. With so many cars parked around the property she expected that someone must be home, but after her second set of knocks the door still didn't open.

She was about to walk away when she heard a shout and some laughter from the backyard. With careful steps, she picked her away around the side of the house. When she peeked around the back corner she saw that there were many lawn chairs, a large fire pit, and a grill in the backyard. At least ten people were gathered around the fire pit. More laughter came from the group.

Blu walked toward the gathering.

"Hi. Sorry to interrupt."

A woman stood up and peered at her. She wore a sleeveless black t-shirt that showed off several intricate tattoos. "Can I help you?"

"My name is Blu. I'm here to speak with Betty."

"I'm Betty." She tilted her head to the side. "But I can't say that I've ever seen you before. I'm sure we haven't met."

"No, I don't think we have. Actually I'm here to tell you some bad news. I'm sorry that it would come at a time of celebration."

"Oh, it's just a little party." She shrugged. "What's the bad news? If it's about the mortgage, I'll be paying it soon."

"No, it's not about that. It's about your ex-husband, George."

"Oh?" She smirked. "What about him?"

Blu shifted from one foot to the other. Somehow, during the minutes leading up to the meeting with Betty, it had never occurred to Blu that she would be the one informing the woman of her ex-husband's death. She suddenly felt underqualified. She took a deep breath and looked Betty in the eyes. "I'm afraid that George passed away this morning."

Betty placed a hand over her face. Her shoulders shook.

Blu's heart sank. She reached out and squeezed Betty's shoulder. "I'm so sorry for your loss."

"Please, don't be." Betty pulled her hand away from her face to reveal that she wasn't crying at all. She was laughing. "What do you think we're celebrating?"

"I'm sorry?"

"Sure. I found out about him a few hours ago. I threw this party together to celebrate the fact that the pain in my rear end no longer exists."

Blu's eyes widened. "Don't you think it's a little harsh

to celebrate someone's death?"

"Not George's. Now what is it that you want?"

"I just wanted to be sure that someone contacted you. I thought maybe you could give me an idea of what George was like."

"Why would you want to know that?"

"Who's this babe?" The man—who, by his size, Blu guessed must have owned the boots on the porch—stepped up beside Betty. "A cute friend you never told me about?"

"Cut it out, Wayne. This is some woman who must have had a thing for George."

"Oh, trust me, you dodged a bullet." Wayne chuckled. "That man wasn't worth the breath in his body."

Blu tried not to let her disgust show. It was hard for her to believe that anyone could be so cruel.

"I understand that you were supposed to meet with him this morning?"

"Sure, at that little cafe by the beach. He finally agreed to work things out so that Wayne and I could make our love legal. Of course, as usual, he was a no-show."

"Because he was dead."

"Whatever—one last disappointment. Anyway, it doesn't matter now. He's dead. I'm a widow, and I get his retirement money. Not too shabby if you ask me." She grinned at Wayne. "It's a bit like winning the lottery, don't you think, honey?"

"Sure is."

Blu bit into her bottom lip. "So you were at the cafe this morning?"

"Just after it opened. We were in the parking lot for a bit before that. You know, enjoying one another's company. That waitress was slow and real snotty when we banged on the door to be let in. She acted like it was such an imposition to be taken away from her prep work. Really, honey, rolling napkins is not that important."

"Well, I guess I should let you get back to your party."

"Want a beer?" Wayne winked at her. "We might not be friends now, but we could be."

"No. No, that's okay." Blu forced a smile. "I have to be going."

She couldn't get to her car fast enough.

CHAPTER 9

Once Blu was settled back in the driver's seat, she knew exactly where she had to go next. Cathy had left out one very important detail about her morning, and Blu wanted to know why. Since the kids were with Maddie, she could spare one extra stop.

She wanted to hear from Cathy what else had happened that morning. With Betty's detailed account, she found it hard to believe that the waitress's description was made up, but Blu wanted to confirm it.

When she arrived at the cafe, it was during the lull between lunch and dinner. She pulled open the door and stepped into a nearly empty restaurant. Cathy turned away from the counter with a coffee pot in her hand. When she saw Blu, she turned right back and started to head for the kitchen.

"Cathy, wait. I just need to speak with you for a minute."

"Are you a customer?" A man with slicked-back hair and a handlebar mustache met her eyes. "She's on the clock."

"Yes. I could use a cup of coffee, please."

"Cathy." The man tilted his head toward an open spot at the counter.

Cathy sighed and walked toward the empty seat.

Blu took the seat in the same moment that Cathy set down a coffee mug rather hard.

"What are you doing back here?" She looked into Blu's eyes.

"Like I said, I need some coffee—and maybe a few more answers from you."

"Look, like I said earlier, I'm not interested in being a witness."

"Have the police come to talk to you?" Blu studied her.

Cathy glanced away.

"They haven't, right? We kept your name out of it."

"Yes. You did, I guess. They haven't been here yet, anyway."

"See? No reason to withhold information."

"What do you mean?"

"I was wondering if you had some early customers this morning."

"Oh. Yes, I did."

"And you didn't think to mention it?"

"Why would I?" She frowned and poured coffee into the mug. "They were just this annoying loud couple. They pounded on the door and demanded to be let in before I was even open for business. I didn't want a disturbance, so I just let them in."

"Were they here before or after you noticed George's friend on the beach?"

"Before. I let them in before I saw him, but they had been in the parking lot for a little while before that. Why do they matter?"

"The woman happens to be George's ex-wife."

"Oh." Cathy's eyes widened. "That makes sense. I heard them arguing back and forth about someone they were supposed to meet. She did say the name George, but you know, there are a lot of Georges in the world."

"Did they seem nervous—or angry?"

"Angry." She shook her head. "Mostly that I didn't have any alcohol to serve them. We don't offer that until lunch."

"What about George? Did she say anything in particular that you can recall?"

"No. I'm sorry. I didn't want to listen in. I was busy, and I was annoyed with them, so I just did my best to ignore them."

"And when they left? Had you seen George's partner yet?"

"Yes. I noticed him before any other customers came in. I wasn't sure what to think. Then I got caught up with the couple. They were irritated then—slammed their money down, ignored me, and stormed out."

"Did you see if they went down to the beach or not?"

"I didn't really pay attention."

"What about anyone else you might have seen that morning? A delivery man? Anyone."

"Why do you want to know? I mean, isn't it clear that George's partner killed him?"

"Witnesses are always helpful, and since you don't want to be involved, finding other witnesses would be ideal."

Cathy seemed to be studying her before she continued. "Are you a cop or something? I thought you were just AJ's girlfriend."

"I'm not his girlfriend." Blu blushed and looked away. "And I'm not a cop either. I'm a nanny, actually. But you should be glad I'm not a cop. If I was a cop, you'd be at the police station looking at mug shots, right?"

"True." Cathy paused. "So back to your question—I didn't see anyone else, except…"

"Except for who?"

"Councilman Carry—but he runs this strip of beach every morning."

"So did you see him this morning?" Blu's heart quickened.

"Sure."

"Before or after you saw George's partner?"

"Before—about twenty minutes before. He runs at the same time every day." She smiled. "Sometimes he waves to me. It's nice to be noticed."

"It's interesting that he would run in this area when he seems very aware of the crime that happens."

"He does it for that reason. He says he won't turn a blind eye to it, and he wants the people of the local area to know that." Cathy smiled a little. "It's actually kind of refreshing to find a politician who wants to be so involved."

"Hm. I guess it is." Blu swirled some milk into her coffee. She tapped the side of the mug. It seemed to her that Cathy had told her everything that she could, but the question in her mind now was, who did that ring belong to? Maybe if she had a picture of it, she could ask. "Did you notice if the couple from this morning had any jewelry on?"

"Are you kidding?" Cathy laughed. "I noticed alright. I've never seen someone wear that much bling and leave such a bad tip."

"Was Betty wearing a ring?"

"No, it wasn't the woman. It was the guy. He looked like he'd knocked over a jewelry store and decided to wear his spoils all in one day. Well, you know why a guy wears a ring on every finger."

"Style?" Blu raised an eyebrow.

"Are you kidding?" Cathy quirked an eyebrow. "Where are you from?"

"Small town USA." Blu frowned.

"Oh, I guess that explains it. Look, you know someone is looking for a fight if they load up their hands with rings. Every punch is made a lot worse when you're wearing armor."

"I get it." Blu's eyes widened. "So you think the guy you saw was looking for a fight?"

"I don't know if he was or not. Some guys wear that kind of stuff just to look tough—all bark and no bite, if you know what I mean. But that guy looked big enough to not need anything else to make him look tough."

Blu recalled the massive size of Wayne. She also remembered that he didn't have any of his rings on when she'd met him. That was a good hint to her that the rings weren't really about style. He'd worn them for a purpose and didn't have them on later in the day. Blu also wondered how Betty had been notified so fast. Was it the police that contacted her, or was it that she had first-hand knowledge that her ex-husband was dead?

"Thanks for the information, Cathy." She left a five-dollar tip for her cup of coffee. It wasn't much, but it was something.

As she stood up from the stool, she noticed a face looking in the front window of the cafe. She only saw it for a second, but she thought perhaps it was the councilman.

She hurried out the door to see if she could catch him.

CHAPTER 10

When Blu stepped outside of the cafe, there was no one in the parking lot. As she walked to her car she called AJ to tell him about her meeting with the ex-wife and with Cathy.

"Blu, I was just about to call you."

"Really?"

"Yes, my uncle let me know that it has been confirmed that George was involved with drugs. In fact, there's a sting operation in place that had surveillance on George and his partner, Xavier Tillman."

"You mean they have the murder on camera?"

"Actually, that's the strange thing. They were pulled off the case this morning. However, they did get wind of Xavier suspecting that George was somehow involved with the police operation."

"Was he?"

"Not as far as my uncle can tell. But you know how these things can be between jurisdictions. No one wants to give out too much information."

"So, Xavier thought that George was going to turn him in to the cops. That's certainly could be motivation to kill him."

"It sure is. The problem is that no one can find Xavier."

"What about the ring?"

"Oh, I forgot to ask about that. I'm sorry."

"That's okay. I just think it could be important." She filled AJ in on what Cathy had told her about Betty and Wayne's visit to the cafe.

"That is interesting, but it sure does seem to be pointing at Xavier as the killer. So I don't think there's too much else to be concerned about—which is a relief, because I'm really looking forward to getting to spend some time with you at the clambake tomorrow."

"I'll have the kids, remember."

"I know." He paused as if he might say something more, but when he spoke it was casual. "Have a good night, Blu."

"Thanks, AJ. You too." She hung up the phone.

For a moment the desire to call him back overwhelmed her, but she pushed it down. This was not the time to start any kind of real conversation. She still hadn't figured out what it was that she wanted, and it wasn't fair to AJ to even bring up the topic without knowing how she felt.

She drove back to Maddie's to pick up the kids.

After updating her friend about the case, Maddie

shook her head. "It seems to me that two criminals did us all a favor. One took out the other. Now Xavier will be in jail and no more drugs can be run through him."

"Maybe." Blu shook her head. "It just seems very strange to me that the surveillance team was pulled the very morning that George was killed."

"A coincidence?"

"Maybe." Blu gathered the kids. "See you tomorrow at the clambake?"

"I'll be there. And so will you—with AJ." Maddie grinned. "Is it going to be the big day?"

"The big day?"

"First kiss, first declaration of love, first promise to have a happily ever after?"

"Maddie, you've been watching those teen romance movies again, haven't you?"

"It's all Chrissa ever wants to watch!" Maddie rolled her eyes. "But look, it could be real life for you. It's the perfect setting, the perfect moment."

"Sure. Right before we return to the reality of Manhattan."

"Blu, you're so stubborn! We live in the age of technology. It's not like you can't video chat, text, and e-mail."

"Hm." Blu tilted her head from side to side. "I don't know, Maddie. Do you ever have that feeling that the choice you make is going to change the rest of your life? Like once you make it, there's no option to go back?"

"Yes." Maddie held Blu's gaze. "Which is why it's imperative that you at least kiss him. You can't spend the rest of your life wondering if he was the one that got away."

"Is that really fair to him, though? What if we kiss and there's nothing between us?"

"Girl, you two can be standing on opposite sides of the room and I have to cut the chemistry between the two of you to get through. Trust me, you shouldn't be worried about there being nothing there, you should be worried about just how powerful it's going to be—because once it starts, there's going to be no stopping it."

"Then maybe that's all the more reason not to let it start."

Maddie sighed and looked into her friend's eyes. "I know what this is about."

"What?" The kids ran past Blu to the car.

"It's because of me, isn't it?"

"Well, Maddie, I love you, but not like that."

"That's not what I mean." Maddie winked at her. "What I meant was, you watched what I went through with my ex. You're scared you're going to face the same thing. But I think it's different with AJ. You can't let my failed romance be the only example of love that you have. So my husband didn't turn out to be the guy I thought he was; that doesn't mean that will be true of every guy that you meet—that either one of us meet, I mean."

Blu smiled sadly. "I hear you Maddie. I think I just

need some time to think about it."

"There isn't much time left, you know."

"I know."

Blu surprised herself with the emotion that Maddie's statement caused her to feel. In her gut, she couldn't imagine being ready to say goodbye to AJ.

CHAPTER 11

Blu drove the kids back to the beach house. Her mind spun with what she'd discovered during her exploration. There was reason to believe that Betty and Wayne had been at the cafe, not only to meet with George but to cause him harm. And now she had to wonder if that face she'd seen earlier in the window really was the councilman.

She was distracted from her thoughts when she parked in the driveway and saw that Rachel's car was there as well.

"Kids, Mom's home." Blu smiled.

Joey and Marley raced for the door. When they pushed through it, Rachel was just on the other side to greet them.

"Hi, my sweethearts!" She hugged them both and kissed their heads. "I was hoping you'd be home soon. I've been looking forward to seeing you all day. Can you go get washed up? Then we'll have dinner and a movie."

"Yes!" Marley hopped up and down.

"I'm getting the bathroom first!" Joey ran down the

hall. Marley shrieked and ran after him.

Rachel shook her head and laughed as she turned back to Blu. "I heard what happened on the beach today. What a shame."

"Don't worry, the kids are okay."

"I'm not worried. I never worry when they're with you." Rachel smiled at her. "Listen, I know I said that you could take the kids to the clambake, but it turns out Marshall is going to be able to be here and help us get packed up for the trip back. So if you don't mind too much, I'd really like for it just to be us and the kids tomorrow."

"That's fine, I don't mind at all. I'm glad that you and Marshall are going to be getting some time together."

"Me too." Rachel offered a blissful smile. "I was starting to think we'd go most of the summer without seeing him. I'm glad he's making an effort to be here for this."

"Well, dinner won't take me long to make unless there's something special you'd like tonight."

"Actually, I can handle dinner. I think someone is waiting for you outside."

"Huh?" Blu glanced out the window. She saw AJ in the driveway.

"I told him that I'd send you out." Rachel smiled. "He's a very sweet guy."

"Seems that way." Blu narrowed her eyes. She wondered if this was his attempt to ambush her and demand answers. "Thanks, Rachel."

"Have fun!"

Blu stepped out into the driveway.

AJ turned to face her and instantly smiled. "Hi. I hope you don't mind me just dropping by."

"Of course not. But I thought I already said—"

"—I know, but I wanted to tell you about something, and Rachel and I arrived at the same time. She told me she was giving you tonight and tomorrow off. I think she had a reason." He smiled shyly.

"I bet she did." Blu shook her head. "What did you want to tell me?"

"I checked into the ring, and it turns out one wasn't found. I thought you might want to take a walk with me and see if we can find it."

Blu smiled. "I think I like that idea. It'll be like a treasure hunt."

"Exactly. I even brought something that will help." He held his hand out to her. "I'm parked right around the corner. I didn't want to take up space in the driveway."

Blu took his hand without realizing what she was doing at first. When she felt the jolt of his skin touching hers, she did her best not to pull back. Maddie's words replayed through her mind.

Together they walked around the corner to the jeep.

"See?" He pointed to the back of his jeep, where he'd stowed a metal detector.

"Perfect! Let's go." Blu walked toward the jeep. It

seemed to her that AJ was watching her every step. She shivered a little as she slid into the passenger seat.

"Cold?" AJ asked as he got into the driver's seat.

"No, I'm fine."

He looked over at her, parted his lips, then seemed to change his mind. He started the engine and they drove toward the area of the beach where the clambake was to be held.

Blu fiddled with the radio the entire time in an attempt to keep conversation at a minimum.

It was a short drive.

When he parked, Blu hopped right out of the jeep with AJ following after her.

"I'm not sure how we're going to be able to see anything. It's getting dark already."

"I have flashlights." AJ glanced over at her. "But you'll have to stay close to me, so that I can use the metal detector. Do you think you'll be able to tolerate being around me that long?"

"AJ." Blu frowned. "That's a silly question."

"Is it?" He rested the metal detector against the side of his jeep and turned to face her. "Are you going to tell me that you haven't been avoiding being alone with me? Are we back to pretending that you don't feel this—this connection between us?"

She could see him trying to meet her eyes, but Blu looked out over the water. The heat of his fingertips brushed along the curve of her shoulder.

"See?"

"I thought we were here to look for the ring?"

AJ was silent, but he picked up the metal detector. He reached into the trunk of the jeep and pulled out a flashlight as well.

"Here you go." He held it out to her.

Blu had to turn back to look at him in order to take the flashlight. She was certain that her cheeks were glowing with a blush in the evening light. When her fingers wrapped around the flashlight, AJ held on to it instead of releasing it.

"Blu?"

She automatically met his eyes in response to his speaking her name. The moment she did, her breath caught in her throat at the intensity of the warmth that filled her senses.

"We're going to have to talk about it sometime." His voice was softened by the intimacy of their visual connection. "I don't want to let this go—without at least knowing what it is that's there between us, I mean."

Her chest ached with a mixture of sympathy and dread. He wanted an answer from her, and he wasn't wrong to ask for it. She still wasn't sure she could offer it.

"We should get started while there's still a little light."

"Fine." AJ released the flashlight and began to walk off across the sand with the metal detector in one hand.

Blu watched him walk away. Every step he took seemed to be in time with the sinking sensation that she was feeling within her.

CHAPTER 12

Blu forced herself to focus on the matter at hand. She wanted the ring. It didn't matter if it wasn't needed to convict Xavier. She still wanted it. After a few moments she fell into step beside AJ. The tension that had carried between them during their conversation faded into a comfortable closeness that Blu had yet to be able to explain.

"When he drew it in the painting, it looked like it was about here." Blu pointed to the sand beside the rowboat.

"You know the tide probably washed it away." AJ waved the metal detector over the wet sand. "But we can still look."

Blu shined the flashlight on the sand and hoped that something would glimmer in the light. Instead, she noticed a shadow. Her stomach twisted as she recognized it as a figure. She looked up toward the cafe and saw a silhouette of a man. The man appeared to be staring down at them.

"AJ!" She nudged his arm with her elbow. "Someone

is watching us."

"Hm?" AJ looked in the direction that Blu pointed. He squinted his eyes. "Who is that? Give me the flashlight."

Blu's hand trembled as she handed it over. Was it Xavier?

AJ waved the beam of light in the direction of the man. When the light skimmed over the figure it was clear who it was.

"Oh boy, we're in trouble." AJ gritted his teeth.

"Maybe he didn't see us?" Blu cringed.

"He saw us." AJ lowered the flashlight as the man walked toward them.

Chief Pitman adjusted his hat as he looked from AJ to the metal detector, then to Blu. "Why does it not surprise me that you're involved in all this, Blu?"

"We're not doing anything wrong. Are we?"

Chief Pitman narrowed his eyes. He placed his hands on his hips.

Blu was quite familiar with his stance. It communicated his displeasure in a way that no words ever could.

"I don't know—is keeping law enforcement out of the loop doing something wrong?"

"Uncle Paul, we're just looking for the ring I told you about."

"Right. Would you like to know why I'm here?"

"Yes." AJ cleared his throat.

"Well, I've been told that there's a potential witness to this crime, but not the name of that witness. Since I can't trust my nephew or his good friend Nanny Blu to tell me the truth, I came out here to see who might have had a view of the rowboat. Surprise, surprise, I figured out that someone in the cafe would be able to see this area of the beach perfectly. I also know that there was only one employee working that early in the morning."

"Chief Pitman, we were only honoring her wishes." Blu frowned. "It's not AJ's fault."

"Oh, indeed it is, because in a murder investigation, no one's wishes matter. Understand?" He studied her for a moment. "Well, no, I guess you wouldn't understand, but let me fill in some blanks for you. If someone dies on my beach, I'm going to find out who did it, why they did it, and who saw it, no matter who stands in my way."

Blu looked away from him. She could feel the frustration in his heavy glare. She didn't want to be faced with the truth about the situation, which was that it might have been better to be honest with the chief from the beginning.

"Uncle Paul, Blu is just trying to help. You know that. Besides, you already know who did it."

"Do I?" He lifted his shoulders in a shrug. "Then you need to tell my suspect that. Because my guys picked up Xavier Tillman this evening at the airport. He was trying to get out of the country."

"That sounds pretty incriminating to me."

"Me too. However, Xavier tells me that he had nothing to do with George's death. He claims that he came here to meet George, but that George was already dead. He took off, because he knew that he'd be blamed for it. He claims that he even left the drugs behind."

"Well, that's not true." AJ set the metal detector down in the sand. "If he left the drugs, the crime scene technicians would have found them."

"Sure, if they were out in the open, or even buried in the sand. But maybe not if they were hidden somewhere else."

"Were they?" Blu looked back at Chief Pitman.

"Yes, actually they were. According to Xavier, they're still right here on the beach. Now, if what he tells me pans out, we have a big problem."

"What's that?" AJ raised an eyebrow.

"I know a lot of things about drug runners. Like, for example, I know that George was the lowest man on a totem pole. Xavier was one step up, but he's got some seriously powerful and dangerous men to answer to. So, even if he killed George, he wouldn't dare to leave the drugs behind. If his boss got wind of it, Xavier would pay the same price that George did."

"I don't understand." Blu shook her head. "If that's the case, then even if Xavier did find George dead, why wouldn't he have taken the drugs?"

"He claims that he couldn't because it was too hard to get to them—that he was afraid he'd draw attention to himself, and he didn't want to face a murder charge. So he fled instead. Not only was he trying to get away from the police, he was also trying to get away from those in charge of him. So let's just say our friend Xavier Tillman is a nervous wreck."

"Then we need to see if the drugs are still here. Where did he say they were?"

"Inside the boat. That's how George would smuggle them. He kept the rowboat attached to his fishing boat. He would hide the drugs inside a false panel in the rowboat. That way if police raided the boat, he could just cut the tie and claim that nothing on the boat was his."

"The drugs are still in this rowboat?" Blu kicked the side of it. "Wouldn't the technicians have found them?"

"Maybe they should have, but they weren't looking for them. I thought I'd check things out for myself, then surprise—I run into the two of you."

"Well, let's take a look, Uncle Paul. I can flip the boat over."

"Go ahead." Chief Pitman took a step back and Blu trained the beam of the flashlight on the boat.

CHAPTER 13

AJ strained for a moment but easily flipped the boat over. It looked like any other rowboat. He knocked on the wooden seats, then Blu noticed his attention shift to the bilge of the boat. "Look at this. Blu, shine the light here." He pointed out a piece of wood that appeared to be shinier than the rest. "It's not even wood." AJ pulled at the corner. "It's like a sticker." He peeled back the sticky paper to reveal a small compartment in the bottom of the boat. Inside was a large package wrapped in dark brown paper, which nearly blended in with the wood.

"Looks like George was smarter than we thought. The surveillance team couldn't figure out how he was bringing the drugs in. Now we know. Don't touch it, AJ!" Chief Pitman snapped.

AJ drew his hand back.

"Fingerprints." His uncle pulled out his phone. "I'll call for someone to collect it."

Blu moved closer to AJ. "What do you think this means about Xavier? Do you think he was telling the truth about George already being dead?"

"I think it's possible." AJ kicked the toe of his shoe into the sand. When he did, something sparkled in the flashlight beam.

"AJ, don't move!" Blu crouched down and pointed at a gold ring that stuck up out of the wet sand. She pulled a tissue out of her pocket and picked the ring up. When she turned the ring toward the flashlight she could see the letters A and L engraved on the flat square surface of the top of the ring.

"It looks almost like a class ring." AJ narrowed his eyes. "But not one that I've seen before. Uncle Paul." He turned to his uncle just as he hung up the phone. "We found the ring."

"Alright." Chief Pitman nodded. "Now we're getting somewhere." He took the ring from Blu and slipped into a small plastic bag. "I'll have this checked out—right after I speak to Cathy Bingham."

Blu met his eyes. "Don't."

"Excuse me?" He folded his arms across his chest.

AJ moved closer to both of them.

"She was terrified." Blu held his gaze and set her jaw. "She's afraid that she's going to get hurt for speaking up. If you go to talk to her, then there could be a problem."

"Listen, I've been doing this little thing called police work for a very long time now. I don't think that you need to tell me how to do it. It's bad enough that the two of you thought it was important to keep her name from me. Did it ever occur to you that without having her name, I have no way of protecting her from someone that might want to harm her—that I might have information that could keep her safe?"

"Not really." Blu shook her head. "She offered us information on the condition that we would keep her identity a secret. I respected her wishes, as did AJ."

"Or he respected yours." Chief Pitman sighed and unfolded his arms. "I understand where you're coming from. But now, more than ever, it's important that I speak to her. She may be our only eyewitness, and that's not something that I can pretend I don't know about."

"Maybe I should go with you?" Blu frowned.

"Not this time, Blu. I promise, I'll be gentle." The chief turned and walked back toward the parking lot.

Blu considered trying to stop him, but she assumed that he'd do what he wanted to do, no matter what.

"I'm sorry, but he does have to do his job." AJ took Blu's hand in his and led her toward the jeep. "I hope you're not too upset."

"I just hope that Cathy will be okay. She's in for a big surprise tonight." She sighed. "I hope she doesn't think that we're the ones who directed him to her."

"There's nothing we can do about it now."

"You're right."

Blu took one last look out over the water. Sometimes the ocean appeared so desolate and lonely to her at night. Without even the moon to trace a path along its darkened surface, it was easy to believe that it was nothing more than a big black hole.

AJ opened the door for her.

She climbed into his jeep and settled back against the seat. That was what the end of summer felt like. It was an unusual feeling for her. Normally she was excited for the change in routine, for getting back to the city and all of the activities that she and the kids enjoyed. Summer was an endless parade of sunscreen, sandy bathing suits, and sticky ice cream faces. It was a bit more work than the school year. But nothing could relieve the sensation of dread that seemed to building within her—nothing but the touch of AJ's hand on the back of hers as he reached out to her.

"You okay? You look like you're a million miles away."

Blu smiled a little. "No, more like just a hundred."

"Okay." He gave her hand a light squeeze. "Try not to let all this get to you, Blu. It's a horrible thing, but it doesn't have to ruin our last day together."

"I don't think anything could." She smiled as she looked at him. "As long as I'm with you."

"What?" His eyes widened. He gasped. "Was that an actual admission that you enjoy spending time with me, Blu? Wait a minute." He pulled out his cell phone. "Let me figure out how to make this thing record, because I need audio proof—"

"Stop it!" Blu laughed and without a single thought about it, she leaned over and kissed his cheek. She heard his sharp breath in reaction to the sudden kiss. Then she felt his cheek move beneath her lips. He caught just the corner of her lips with his own before she pulled away.

MACI GRANT

CHAPTER 14

A thick tension filled the jeep as Blu stared straight forward through the windshield.

AJ pulled his hand away and started the engine. He glanced over at her. "I'm sorry. I didn't mean to make you uncomfortable." He shifted the car into gear and began the drive back to the beach house.

A million things rushed through Blu's mind. She knew he was waiting for her to say something, but she had no idea what to say. As confused as she was afraid she was making him with her mixed signals, she was even more confused.

AJ stopped the jeep at the base of the driveway. He left the engine on. When he looked over at her, she noticed the strain in his expression.

"Blu, we really need to talk about things."

"I agree. I think it's interesting that the drugs were left behind. Do you think that whoever killed George didn't even know they were there?"

AJ stared at her for a long moment.

A part of her expected that he'd demand an

explanation from her. Instead, he coughed and rubbed the curve of his chin.

"It's possible. We've all been assuming that this was a drug-related murder, but what if it wasn't? What if it's more personal? Maybe Wayne had more to do with it than he's claiming. They were right here at the time of the murder, so we can't overlook them both as suspects."

"That's true, but Cathy was with them. At least, once they knocked on the door of the cafe," said Blu.

"And before?"

"Betty claimed they were having some fun in the parking lot." Blu wiggled her eyebrows.

"Oh?" AJ grinned. "Well, that's one way to kill time, I guess. But it also leaves a window of time when they weren't seen by anyone. It's possible they went down to the water and took care of their problem."

"Wait a minute—they went down on to the mud flats, wouldn't they have mud on their shoes?"

"Maybe they tossed them."

Blu recalled the boots she'd seen on the porch of the house. "I may have an idea of how to find out."

"As long as that idea doesn't interfere with the clambake tomorrow." AJ reached out and gave her hand a squeeze. "I'm really looking forward to it."

"Me too." Blu smiled. "Also, it will just be us. Rachel and Marshall are going to take the kids to the clambake, so she gave me the day off."

"Wow." He grinned and leaned a little closer to her.

"So, we're going to be alone? Together?"

"Along with everyone else at the big bash." Blu winked at him.

"Oh, trust me—to me, no one else in the world will exist." He spoke each word in a serious tone.

"You're such a sweet-talker." Blu rolled her eyes.

She opened the car door. Before she could step out, AJ grabbed her by the hand. She turned back with surprise and for an instant she was certain that he was about to pull her in for a kiss.

He traced his thumb along the back of her hand. Then he raised her hand to his lips and placed a soft kiss just above her knuckles. Blu shivered and pulled her hand away.

She caught sight of AJ's pleased smile just before she jumped out of the jeep. It didn't matter how much she tried to deny it; the moment that he touched her, the evidence was there.

AJ waved to her as he drove off down the street.

CHAPTER 15

Blu walked up to the house as her head spun. The house was dark, so she slipped in quietly. She didn't want to disturb the kids or Rachel. They had a big day the next day, and she knew that the kids probably had a hard time going to sleep with the excitement of their father's arrival.

She started down the hall toward her room. As she passed the living room, she heard the clink of a glass being set down on the coffee table. She froze. Was Rachel still up? She peeked into the dimly lit living room and recognized Marshall right away. He sat on the couch with only a small lamp on for light.

"Oh, I'm sorry Marshall, I didn't know that you were home."

"Hey, Blu. It's okay. I'm sorry if I surprised you. I got in about an hour ago, and everyone's gone to bed. I'm a little off schedule from the flight."

"I'm so glad that you were able to make it for the clambake."

"Me too." He sighed and picked up his glass.

Blu lingered by the entrance of the living room. As a

rule of thumb, she tended to be less friendly with the husbands of the couples she worked for. She knew it made the wives feel more at ease, and there wasn't often much she needed to do that involved the father of the children. But Marshall was a little different. He was rarely home, but when he was, he usually spent all of his time with the kids. As a result, Blu got to know him a little better than most. Despite the dim lighting, the slump of his shoulders and the tenor of his voice indicated to Blu that he was as sad as Rachel often looked.

"Can I get you anything, Marshall? There's ice cream in the freezer."

"No. I'm fine." He finished his drink and set the glass down. "So the body at the beach—it's all over the news. Do you know anything about that?"

"Only that it might involve drugs." She decided not to mention that she'd seen the drugs herself that very night.

Marshall sighed and slouched back against the couch. "You know, I thought being wealthy was all that was needed."

"What do you mean?"

He shook his head. "I wanted to be a good dad—you know, protect my kids from everything. I thought if I made enough money, they'd always be safe—that I'd never have to worry—but that's not the case, is it?" He glanced over at her.

"I think you're a great dad."

"Thanks, Blu, I appreciate that. One day when you have your own kids, you'll understand. Nothing I do will ever make up for the time that I've missed with them. I keep telling myself that I'm making the smart decisions by following my career—by providing for them, rather than taking time to be with them, but the truth is, I've been missing out. I hope to change that over the next year. I want to be here for my family, even if I can't make up for the past."

"I know that they'll all love that." Blu smiled warmly at him.

"Blu, I know that you're an adult, and I know that you have your own family to guide you, but can I share some advice with you?"

"Sure." Blu sat down on the arm of the couch.

"If you have the opportunity to experience life, then experience it. Even if it seems messy or risky. In the long run, it's worth it to take that risk. It's worth it not to always make the smart decision. Otherwise, you end up in your forties with very little life lived and no idea what the future will hold."

Blu sensed his deep regret. She longed to be able to show him just how much his wife and kids adored him, but she knew that was something only they could do.

"I'll remember that. I promise. Thank you, Marshall. Try to get some sleep, okay?"

"Yes, I will. You too."

Blu stood up and walked to her room. Marshall's

words stuck with her even as she changed into a nightshirt.

Was she doing what he'd talked about? Or was she only making the safe choices in her life?

She'd fled the opportunity to become a journalist when the job seemed too dangerous. She gave up on dating before she'd even tried, because she thought if it wasn't the right man, it wasn't worth the risk or the time. But how would she ever know who was the right man when she never gave any of them a chance?

She sat down on the edge of her bed and pulled off her shoes. There was a lot of time stretched out ahead of her and there was one conclusion that she'd come to.

She didn't want to spend that time alone.

Her fingertips touched the corner of her lips. What would have happened if she hadn't pulled away from AJ earlier? Would the sky have fallen? Would the earth have crumbled away beneath her? Maybe she was being silly to think one little kiss could matter so much.

CHAPTER 16

As Blu stretched out on her bed, she tried to distract herself with thoughts about the case. If Xavier wasn't the murderer, then who was? Wayne? Someone else? Her mind drifted back to the face she'd seen in the window of the cafe.

James Carry. It was a long shot, but he was on the beach that morning. Even if he wasn't involved in the crime, that didn't mean that he didn't know something.

She sat up and grabbed her phone. Without even thinking about the time, she called Maddie.

"Hello?" Her friend's sluggish voice made Blu look at the clock. It was nearly midnight.

"Oh, I'm so sorry to wake you. This can wait until the morning. Go back to sleep."

"It's okay. What's up?"

"I was wondering if you could look into someone for me—but I can call you back in the morning."

"No, it's okay. I'm up." She cleared her throat. "Who is it?"

"Councilman James Carry."

"Oh wow, a heavy hitter, huh? Do you really want me to shake that tree? You never know what might fall out."

"I'm just curious. His name keeps coming up. I wonder if he might know something more about what happened at the beach than what he's been talking about."

"Sure, I'll look into him." Maddie paused. "Are you doing okay, Blu?"

"Yes. We had some interesting developments in the case tonight." She filled Maddie in on what they'd found. "I'm just not sure what to think any more. I thought all this was settled—that Xavier was the killer—but now that we found the drugs left behind, it's harder to believe that."

"Well, Wayne had plenty of motive, and he and Betty sure aren't hiding the fact that they're quite happy about George's death," said Maddie.

"That's true. Plus, they were there. And Cathy mentioned that Wayne wore a lot of rings that day."

"Yes, so the ring you found tonight might be his."

"But, here's the thing. George was drowned in the mud. He wasn't beaten up. Why would Wayne wear all those rings if he was just going to drown him?"

"I don't know. Maybe it seemed like the easier choice. Violence doesn't usually work out the way you plan it."

"Maybe. What a horrible thing to think about before bed. I'm sorry I woke you up to talk about this."

"Yes, I can think of much better things to think about and talk about—like telling AJ that you're willing to give it a go…"

"Maddie!"

"You're thinking about better things now, aren't you?" Maddie giggled.

"Yes. Yes, I am." Blu sighed and hung up the phone.

As she drifted off to sleep, her thoughts turned to her confusion over AJ. It was strange that a murder seemed easier to solve than a romance that hadn't even begun.

Blu woke with a start the next morning. Her heart lurched, then began to pound. For some reason it seemed as if someone had just been in the room with her. She sat up and looked around her bedroom. The morning light was just starting to spill through the window. There was no evidence of anyone else in the room.

When her heart settled, she climbed out of bed and grabbed her robe. She walked to the window. Her room had a partly obstructed view of the beach and the water. She could see the waves as they thrashed against the shore. Maybe the sound of the rough surf had drawn her from her slumber.

Still, she was unsettled. When she looked at the clock she saw that it too early for the kids to be up. She decided to go for a run along the beach. With so much weighing on her mind, a run was the best way for her to sort through it.

Within a few minutes she'd changed out of her pajamas into running gear. She let herself out through the back door. Since Marshall and Rachel had given her the day off, she didn't bother to leave a note.

CHAPTER 17

As Blu ran across the sand, a familiar elation billowed through her. The wind against her face always teased her into believing that she could fly. She ran without really thinking about how far or in which direction she was going.

As the morning progressed she noticed more runners on the beach. One runner in particular appeared to be headed straight for her. Blu moved to the side to give him plenty of room to run past. Still, he seemed to be determined on a collision course with her. She moved again—so close to the water that her shoes almost got wet. He moved as well and continued to run straight for her.

Her heart jumped into her throat as she realized who the runner was—Councilman James Carry.

Why would he be running somewhere completely different than his usual run?

Only then did she realize that she was the one who had gravitated back to the crime scene. She looked over at the cafe that overlooked the stretch of beach she ran across. This was where James Carry ran every morning, according to Cathy, but that didn't explain why he insisted on running straight toward her.

Blu could see that the councilman was wearing wrap-around dark sunglasses. As he got closer, she couldn't tell if he was staring at her or not, but it sure felt like he was.

As he continued in her direction, Blu's heart began to race. Did he somehow know that she had Maddie looking into him?

Just when she thought he was going to run straight into her, Blu jumped into the water. As the salty liquid soaked through her sneakers, James Carry ran right past her as if he'd never seen her in the first place. He didn't offer an apology or an explanation. Blu felt invisible to the man, who obviously thought he was quite powerful.

She waded out of the water and stared after him as he continued to run down the beach. His muscles rippled, revealing his athleticism. A shiver carried along her spine despite the warmth of the morning. Something about him left her feeling very unsettled.

Blu was about to follow him when her cell phone rang. She pulled it out of the case on her hip.

"Hello?"

"Blu, it's Maddie. Are you okay? It sounds like you're panting."

"I was out for a run."

"Oh, sorry to interrupt!"

"No, no. You're fine. Did you find something on James Carry?"

"Something doesn't even begin to describe it. It turns out that James Carry has quite an inflated ego. He seems to think that he can change the entire criminal scene. Not only that, but he's verbally lashed out at the police department, Chief Pitman, and every defense attorney in this town. I dug a little deeper into the community boards, and I found out that he's been posting in crime forums. He's been trying to organize a private security group to patrol the beaches. Some of these posts are really pushing the boundaries of taking the law into your own hands."

"Interesting." Blu squinted into the distance until she couldn't see James any more. "I think we might just have a new suspect to focus on."

"I think you might be right. But Blu, you need to let Chief Pitman handle this one. You know that I'm usually on your side when it comes to investigations, but you're talking about a powerful, influential man here. You can't just go around accusing someone like this of murder. Besides, just because James is an angry vigilante, that doesn't mean that he went as far as murder."

"You're right. But it doesn't mean that he didn't. Every time I think this case is about to be settled, it takes a new twist. I wonder if we'll figure it out before it's time to head back to Manhattan."

"Good question. My family is leaving on Saturday,

what about yours?"

"I'm not sure yet. Marshall is here so I'm guessing it will be sooner rather than later."

"Have you talked to AJ yet?"

"You mean since last night?" Blu laughed. "No, not yet."

"You need to figure things out with him, Blu."

"I know, I know. But first I think I need to talk to Cathy again."

"Sounds like a plan. Where do you want to meet at the clambake?"

"Actually, Rachel and Marshall gave me the day off, so I'm going to go with AJ."

"Great! That's perfect. A romantic day together—"

"—Investigating a murder."

"Oh, Blu, open your mind. At least hold his hand."

"I might hold his hand."

"Good girl."

"Speaking of hands…if you get bored, could you see if you can find a photograph online of James Carry's hands? That ring we found at the crime scene might not belong to Wayne. It could be the councilman's."

"Sure, that shouldn't be too hard to find. Politicians are always shaking hands."

"Thanks, Maddie."

"Good luck today."

Blu smiled as she hung up the phone, but her smile faded when she noticed the footprints the councilman had left in the mud. It made her wonder if he'd left the same prints beside George's body.

She drew a deep breath and began the long run back.

By the time she reached the beach house she'd been out for almost two hours. She was exhausted from the run.

As she stepped into the house, she noticed the remaining scent of French toast. The quiet indicated that the family had already left for the clambake.

Blu was relieved, as it meant that she could take a long hot shower without worrying about being interrupted by the kids.

CHAPTER 18

Blu shed her running clothes and stepped into the shower. As the hot water soothed her muscles, she closed her eyes. Within an instant, she was on the beach again beside the rowboat. She saw Betty and Wayne a few feet away. There was Xavier right next to the boat. When she looked away from Xavier she saw James Carry. He was jogging toward her with those dark sunglasses on. It amazed her that George, a man who'd barely made an impact on the world around him, had three people who despised him enough to want to kill him.

She opened her eyes and let the water run back through her hair. If there was a killer on the loose, she wished there was a way to resolve it before the clambake. There were still a few hours before the actual festivities started. In that time frame, she hoped to question Cathy and check out Wayne's boots.

But there was something else weighing on her mind as well—AJ.

She turned the water off and stepped out of the shower. With a hand towel she wiped the fog away from the mirror. When she gazed at her own reflection, she thought about what he must see in her eyes. She often felt as if she could read his every emotion in the subtle changes of his eyes.

Could he do the same with her? If so, what did he see?

She was sure that he was frustrated over the mixed signals she was sending. A part of her wondered if she'd been throwing herself into this murder investigation as a way to avoid the truth.

Summer was about to end, and Blu had no idea what to do about the intense connection that she'd been feeling with AJ. Could she really just let it go? Or would she make the wrong decision and end up regretting it for the rest of her life?

She continued to think about it as she dressed.

Finally, she grabbed her phone. There was only one way to figure everything out. She needed to immerse herself in the situation, rather than continue her inclination to avoid it.

She dialed AJ's number. The moment she heard his voice, her heart skipped.

"Morning, beautiful."

"Morning. Do you want to go to breakfast with me?"

"I would love to go to breakfast with you. I'm honored that you're asking. When do you want me to pick you up?"

"I'll pick you up."

"I'm at the Beach Bum doing some paperwork."

"No problem, I'll meet you there."

"Okay."

"Say in about ten minutes?"

"I don't know if that will give me enough time to get pretty for you."

Blu smiled at AJ's teasing. "Hm, alright—fifteen."

They both laughed as she hung up the phone.

Blu grabbed her purse and walked out the door. She wanted to find out exactly what Cathy knew about the councilman, because she had a suspicion that it was more than what she'd been saying.

As she started to walk toward her car, the hair on the back of her neck prickled. She paused in the middle of the driveway and looked around. There was no sign of anyone else. Maybe a light breeze had tickled a curl of her still-damp hair. What else could it be? She was alone. Or, she should have been.

She heard the snap of bubble gum. When she turned toward the sound, she was greeted by the sight of a woman not far from the side of the house. Her black leather vest and fierce gaze aided Blu's recognition of her right away.

"Betty, what are you doing here?"

Betty sneered at Blu as she walked toward her.

The closer she came, the more Blu wanted to run.

"I heard that you've been snooping around my Wayne. The cops are all over him now. Why are you trying to ruin things for us?"

"I'm not. I think the police are just investigating the crime. If Wayne wasn't involved, then you have nothing to worry about."

"Oh, really? Then why did the police come talk to him and take him into custody? You must have told them that we were at the cafe that morning."

"Listen, I only told them what you told me. It's nothing they wouldn't have found out on their own." Blu clenched her jaw and did her best not to show any fear. The truth was, she had no idea what Betty might do.

"I waited a long time to find the right man. Wayne is it. Now you're trying to get him taken away. That's not okay with me."

"There's nothing I can do. Unless you have a way to prove that he had nothing to do with it." Blu raised an eyebrow. "Do you?"

"Sure I do. I know he didn't do it. He was with me the whole time."

"That doesn't exactly work as an alibi. You stood to gain the most from your ex-husband's death, and you made public threats against him. Not only that, but after you discovered he was dead, you threw a party. I don't think you can blame the police for being suspicious about that."

"Yes, I celebrated—like any ex-wife would. That's not a crime. Besides, I'm not the only one who saw him in the parking lot with me. There was another guy in the parking lot. I know he saw us, because he glared at us through the car window. It really ruined the moment."

"What did he look like?"

"Isn't that the cops' job? Asking me all these questions? You just tell them what I saw and leave it at that. Understand?"

"It might be better if it were coming from you. I can give you the number of the police station," said Blu.

"No way, nohow. You're not getting me anywhere near any police station." Betty stuck her finger close to Blu's nose. "You started this, you fix it—or I promise you'll pay the price. Wayne better be released in time for the clambake. We have plans today."

"I'm going to pay the price?" Blu narrowed her eyes. "Like George did? He ruined your happily ever after by not finalizing the divorce, didn't he? So you thought you had every right to make sure he never had the chance to live another day."

Betty laughed and coughed at the same time. "George couldn't ruin something if he tried. That man never did a single thing right in his life—aside from dying. Now that he's gone, my life is better. That doesn't make me a murderer, and it doesn't make Wayne a murderer either."

"Maybe not, but that's for the police to decide, not me."

"It seems to me that you have an in with the police. At least that's what I've heard." Betty crossed her arms. "Is that so?"

"I don't think I'd say that. I'm familiar with the police chief, if that's what you mean."

"Sure. Familiar. More like, always hanging around his nephew. AJ, right?"

Blu stared at the woman. She had no idea how she would know anything about AJ. "Yes, that's his name. We're friends."

"Right. Friends. Okay. Well, tell your friend that he better make sure his uncle stays out of my business. I know people in this town too. They might not have badges, but they sure do have guns. Got it?"

"Are you threatening me?" Blu took a slight step back. "Are you aware that's a crime, Betty? Wayne might get released, but if you keep it up you're going to be the one that goes to jail."

"I'm not afraid of you. I don't know how I can make that any more clear to you. And yes, I am threatening you, and yes, you should be afraid of me—very afraid." With that Betty brushed past her and walked down the driveway.

Blu watched her until she got into her car.

CHAPTER 19

Blu waited until she was sure that Betty was gone before getting into her car. It left her unnerved to think that Betty was able to figure out where she lived. What if Rachel and the kids had been home when she'd turned up? Rachel would have been upset and Blu would have been more upset than she already was. If Betty felt comfortable enough to threaten Blu, then what else was she capable of doing? Blu hoped that Chief Pitman would be able to get some information out of Wayne while he held him for questioning.

As she drove to the Beach Bum she tried to shake off the fear that she was feeling. Between her encounter with James Carry on the beach and her run-in with Betty, she had to consider that the case had become quite dangerous.

Blu pulled her car up outside of the Beach Bum. She noticed AJ's jeep was the only vehicle in the parking lot. Still, when she got out she did so with caution. With Betty around, she had no idea what the woman might decide to do.

She hurried to the front door, but when she pulled on the knob, the door was locked. She knocked hard on the door.

AJ opened it a moment later. "Sorry, I was in the back." He frowned as he looked into her eyes. "I thought someone was back there."

"Well, someone was in my driveway this morning when I left to come here—Betty."

"Are you serious? How did she find you? What did she want?"

"To threaten me. She was quite upset about the fact that Wayne was taken into custody this morning. I'm not sure what she's planning, but I don't trust her. She seems to know a lot about you and your uncle."

AJ looked across the empty parking lot toward the beach. His jaw clenched. "Maybe we should skip the clambake then." He shoved his hands into his pockets. "I wouldn't want you to be in danger."

"No way, we're not skipping it. I can't wait to get there. I have a feeling that this clambake is going to be the most eventful one so far."

"Why is that?" AJ followed her to her car.

"Because there's something in the air. Whoever did this to George isn't going to be able to keep it a secret forever."

AJ opened her car door for her and then walked around to the passenger side. "Where are we going for breakfast?"

"It's a surprise." Blu started the car and drove toward the cafe.

When she pulled into the parking lot, AJ sighed and leaned his head back against the seat.

"Why do I get the feeling that this is a working breakfast?"

"Maybe because it is." Blu smiled. "I want another crack at Cathy. I think she's hiding something."

"Why do you think that?"

"Because James Carry is a creep and she failed to mention that."

"Why do you think he's a creep? He doesn't seem so bad."

"He seemed pretty bad to me today when he ran me off the beach into the water."

"What?" AJ paused on the sidewalk and met her eyes. "What are you talking about?"

"I went for a run this morning and happened to end up in his territory. When he ran toward me, I kept trying to move out of his way. He kept trying to get in my way. Let's just say my sneakers ended up wet."

"Wow. That's nuts. Why do you think he did that?"

"I'm not sure. But I want to know what Cathy actually knows about the man."

AJ opened the door to the cafe. When they stepped inside, they were greeted by a packed restaurant. Blu hadn't even thought about the proximity of the cafe to the clambake, or that it would be so busy. She searched the staff for any sign of Cathy.

A frazzled waitress walked up to her.

"It's going to be awhile, unless you two want to sit at the counter."

"That's fine." AJ glanced at Blu. "Right?"

"Sure. Is Cathy available?"

"Oh please, do not even speak that name!" The woman—whose nametag said Heather—waved her hand in the air. "Cathy was supposed to open this morning and didn't bother to show up."

"Is she sick?"

"Who knows?" Heather shrugged. "But this is not the day to bail on the rest of us. I think the entire town is in here for breakfast. Do you two want a menu?"

AJ turned to Blu. "Why don't we just go down to the Gas and Go and get a couple of doughnuts and coffee?" He looked back at the crowd. "I don't think we could even have a decent conversation here."

"Okay, that's a good idea." Blu took his hand and led him back out of the cafe.

CHAPTER 20

Once outside the cafe, Blu began to pace back and forth.

AJ leaned back against the exterior of the cafe and watched her. "What are you thinking?"

"What if something happened to her—to Cathy? What if Betty went after her?"

"Why would Betty do that?"

"I don't know. But Betty said there was a man in the parking lot that saw her and Wayne together in her car. She insisted that she and Wayne had nothing to do with the murder."

"Then they shouldn't have a reason to worry about it. I'm sure that Cathy is just fine. She probably didn't want to deal with the chaos."

"Wait a minute. Didn't your uncle go to talk to her last night?"

"He said he was going to after we left the beach."

"Can you call him and see if he actually spoke with her? If he saw her and she was sick, that would make more sense."

"Sure, I can call him." AJ pulled his phone out of his pocket.

As he dialed the number, Blu kept an eye on the people coming and going throughout the parking lot.

"Hi, Uncle Paul. Yes, I'm with Blu. Oh you didn't?" He glanced over at Blu. "He didn't find anything on the ring yet."

Blu nodded. "Ask him about Wayne. Is he still being held?"

"Blu said you picked up Wayne this morning. Do you still have him? Oh, really?" He looked over at Blu. "They had to release him because they didn't have anything to hold him on."

Blu frowned. "Ask him about Cathy."

"Okay, well, I have a question for you. When you spoke to Cathy last night did she seem ill to you?"

He paused then covered the mouthpiece. "She wouldn't even let him in the door. She refused to answer."

"Did he actually see her?"

"Uncle Paul, I'm going to put you on speakerphone." He pushed a button on his cell phone and held it out for Blu to hear.

"I saw her through the window. When she saw me, she pulled the curtains. I pounded on the door. I threatened to arrest her, but she refused to open it. I was planning to catch her at work today."

"Well, that's not going to happen because she's not here." Blu sighed. "She called in sick. But now I'm guessing that she isn't sick."

"Probably not. She probably thinks I'll be there to talk to her today. Well, maybe I'll swing by her place again then."

"Good idea." Blu nodded.

"I'll let you know what I find."

"Wait, Uncle Paul."

AJ turned off the speaker and put the phone to his ear.

Blu looked at him curiously. "What are you doing?"

"I want you to run a check on James Carry. Yes, the councilman." He frowned. "No, a real check. Blu saw him this morning and something didn't feel right. I trust her instincts. Okay, great. Thank you." AJ hung up the phone and turned to look at Blu.

"You didn't have to do that."

"I think it's important. If he ran you off the beach on purpose then he was trying to intimidate you. If he was willing to intimidate you like that, then who knows what else he'd do to make his point?"

"But why me? Why would he be coming after me?"

"I guess just because we've been asking questions."

"So you think he is involved?"

"I have no idea." AJ sighed. "Every time I think we have a good grasp on what happened to George, something changes."

"I know one way to get to the bottom of it."

"What's that?"

"We start eliminating suspects. If we can narrow it down, we might get to the truth."

"How do you plan to do that?" He winced. "Maybe I shouldn't have asked that."

""I'm glad you did, AJ." Blu smiled as she gestured toward the car. "Care to join me for another ride?"

"Where to?" He shook his head. "Never mind. I shouldn't bother to ask. The answer will be yes no matter where you want to go."

"Then get in."

Blu drove toward Betty's house.

For the better part of the drive AJ gazed out the window. He rubbed his fingertips along the curve of his knee and flicked his fingernails.

Blu wondered if all his nervous behavior was because of her.

"So what's your favorite thing to do in Manhattan?" AJ asked suddenly.

She slowed the car as she prepared to turn into the neighborhood that Betty lived in. "There are too many things to count, really. There's one particular place I like to go when I'm alone. It's a small park. Not huge like Central Park, just big enough to have a few benches and some swings. But there's a short trail that wraps around the entire property. When I walk that trail it reminds me of home."

He looked over at her and smiled. "You must really miss your family."

"Many times I do. We stay in touch, but it's not the same as being face-to-face with someone." She cleared her throat as she realized her mistake.

Her words fell flat between them.

CHAPTER 21

Blu was relieved when she saw the house before them. She parked in front.

"I don't know if we should be doing this." AJ shook his head.

"We know that Betty is in town. Let's see if Wayne is too. If not, maybe we can get a look at his boots. There's no reason for them to be muddy, right?"

"Blu, I think that you're grasping at straws. If my uncle knew that we were doing this—"

"—But he doesn't." Blu met his eyes across the car. "Either we sit back and do nothing—while waiting for Cathy's body to show up somewhere—or we look into things. She trusted us, AJ, remember? She thought that telling us would be a safe choice. Instead, she seems to have dropped off the face of the earth with no hint as to where she might be. So maybe this is a silly thing to do—maybe it won't lead to anything—but I still think that we need to do it."

"If it's what you want, then I'll do it. I understand why you're worried; I just think making a rash decision right now isn't going to be the best course of action. What if Wayne is waiting for us?"

"What if he is?" She shrugged. "As far as he knows, we've just dropped in for a visit. We're not doing anything wrong by stopping by someone's home. Are we?"

"No. I guess not." He shot her a half-smile. "You really can convince me of anything, can't you?"

"It seems that may be true." Blu winked.

AJ reached out and caught the curve of her chin with his finger and thumb.

She was startled as he met her eyes with a determined expression.

"So why can't I do the same to you?"

Blu's lips parted, though she had no idea what words might spill out.

Before she could speak, the front door of the house slammed open. Wayne stomped out in nothing but a pair of flip-flops and a Speedo.

Blu's eyes widened as he charged straight for the car.

AJ's shoulders tensed. He released her chin and started to open the door.

To Blu's surprise, Wayne didn't even seem to notice them. Instead, he ran straight toward a vehicle that appeared to be waiting for him.

"So you thought you were going to leave me behind while you went to the beach, huh?" He climbed into the waiting car, which Blu recognized as belonging to Betty.

As the car sped off, Blu sighed with relief. "I guess now we know no one is home."

"And that Wayne makes very poor choices when it comes to bathing suits."

"Good point." Blu laughed. "Let's go take a look, shall we?"

"Sure. But you have to promise to stay with me. No taking off without telling me where you're going, okay?"

"I think I can agree to that."

"You think, or you do?" AJ studied her.

"I do." She smiled and opened the door to the car. "Let's go."

Blu made her way up the front walk to the porch. AJ followed right behind her. As she hoped, the large boots were still beside the door.

"I don't know if we should touch them. We might corrupt the evidence." AJ paused beside her.

"I'm not worried about it right now. Look." She pointed to the mud that caked the edges and toes of the boots. "Where do you think that came from?"

"I agree that it looks suspicious, but we also can't be sure that it's from the mud flats. There are plenty of places around here where the mud could come from."

"Maybe the medical examiner can test it?" Blu picked up one of the boots and snapped a picture of the mud-caked sole with her cell phone. "It might help get a conviction."

"I doubt it. I mean, there's no way to prove it. Sure, it

might be mud that matches the mud at the mud flats, but that's going to be the same mud found all over the beach."

"You're not being very helpful right now." Blu raised an eyebrow at him.

"I'm sorry." He grinned. "Yes Blu, you're a genius and we've solved the crime. Is that better?"

"It would be, if you'd said it in a more convincing tone." Blu laughed. "Okay, so the boots aren't going to get us the conviction. Why don't we take a look around inside?"

"What?" AJ crossed his arms. "You mean like break in?"

"I mean that the front door doesn't look like it was properly closed, does it?" She tilted her head toward the door that was still slightly open. "It wouldn't be hard to just have a look."

"Blu, that's really crossing a line. My uncle—"

"—Isn't here." Blu grabbed his hand.

"What are you doing?"

"I promised not to take off without you, so you have to come with me." She tugged him forward.

"Wait, wait. Let's think this through for just a minute."

"Oops, sorry. I already opened the door." Blu nudged the door all the way open. "It's too late to think it through now, isn't it?"

"Blu!" He started to tug back on her hand, but Blu

grabbed the doorframe. "Oh wow, you're unbelievable." He rolled his eyes.

"What if Cathy is tied up in there somewhere? What if she needs our help? We have to at least look."

AJ sighed with a force that involved his entire body. "Fine, but we have to make it quick."

"As you wish." She winked at him and turned back to the door.

CHAPTER 22

When Blu pushed through the door of the house, she found herself swamped by an assortment of what she considered junk. Perhaps the beer can sculptures, battery-operated dancing toys, and various football statues were not junk to Betty and Wayne, but Blu saw no purpose to them. The house was in general disarray—clutter mingled with garbage to create a mess.

"I don't know what you expect to find in here, but I'm not interested in digging through it."

"Me either." Blu used the toe of her shoe to lift up a piece of newspaper. A few roaches scuttled off when they were exposed to the light. "Ugh." She shuddered. "Maybe you were right about this being a bad idea."

"Maybe not. Look at this." AJ pointed to a large banner on the wall above what appeared to be the kitchen. It was gold and red, with the letters A and L emblazoned on the material.

"What do you think the letters stand for?"

"Maybe a college, or a club?"

"Let me get a good picture of it." Blu started to step

back in an attempt to get a clear photograph with her phone. When she did, she bumped into the corner of a small side table. The table tilted enough to spill its stack of junk mail. "Oops. I'd better get that. They might know someone was here if I don't."

"Do you really think they'll be able to notice?" AJ scrunched up his nose.

"Maybe not. But some people know where every pile is, even if it's a wreck. I'd rather not risk it." She scooped up the envelopes and papers. As she put them back down on the table, she noticed the top piece of paper in the pile. "Hm. This is interesting." She picked it up and began reading it out loud. "Final notice of foreclosure."

"They're about to lose the house."

"Yes, they are." Blu tapped a fingertip against the letter. "This is motive."

"How so? I doubt that a man like George had life insurance."

"He probably didn't, but he did have a retirement fund. That fund is now going to go to Betty."

"Because their divorce was never legal."

"Exactly. Maybe Betty and Wayne figured out that if they got rid of George they'd get another income."

"But then why bother to set up the meeting? Why allow the waitress to see them?"

"Maybe they thought they were creating an alibi somehow."

"Maybe." AJ shook his head. "Something just doesn't

seem to add up about all this." He glanced over his shoulder in the direction of the door. "And I don't think we should stay here much longer. It sounds like there's a car driving back and forth out there."

"You're right. We don't want to be in here too long. I think we've found everything we can anyway." Blu pushed a few piles of trash out of the way to get to the door.

AJ followed after her. "I don't see any car now. Maybe it was just me being paranoid."

"Either way, it's time to get out of here." As Blu stepped down from the porch her foot rolled forward off the edge of the step. She gasped as she started to fall. The force of AJ's strong arm wrapped around her and kept her upright.

"You okay? Did you twist it?"

"I think I'm okay." Blu noticed that AJ didn't let her go. She also did not try to pull away. She had to admit that it was quite cozy to be tucked into his arms.

The moment her muscles began to relax and she started to tilt her head up toward his, she was startled out of the fantasy that she'd stumbled into.

"Thanks, I'm okay." She pulled away from him.

His fingertips trailed along the slope of her arm as she started to walk toward the car. She felt his presence just behind her until she reached it. Something had to be done to break the tension. Once they were inside the car she started the engine.

"I don't know about you, but I'm still hungry."

"Oh, is this the part where I actually get that date you offered me?"

"It wasn't a date, just breakfast."

"Hm." AJ looked out through the window. "Sure, we wouldn't want to make that mistake."

"I didn't say it would be a mistake. I just meant—it wasn't officially a date."

"How do you make it official? Do you have to apply for a license or something? Maybe it has something to do with getting a signature from a judge?"

"Ha ha, very funny."

He looked over at her with a quirked eyebrow. "I'm serious. Trying to get a date with you feels more like applying for the FBI. Why is that?"

Blu turned down the street that led back toward the beach. "I'm sure it's not that bad."

"That doesn't answer the question. Maybe if you told me the truth—if you were just clear with me—I could stop hounding you."

"Maybe I like you hounding me." She glanced over at him.

"That still doesn't answer the question."

Blu turned into the parking lot of the convenience store. "Maybe that's because I'm hungry. Would you like to get an official doughnut with me?"

"Does it come with an official coffee?"

"That could be arranged."

"What about an official answer to my question?"

"You're not going to let this go, are you?" Blu let her hand linger on the door of the car.

"Not likely."

"You know, I'm starting to think—like uncle, like nephew."

"I'll take that as a compliment." He smirked and popped his door open. "But, that's still not an answer." He met her at the door of the shop and held it open for her.

As they looked over their pastry options Blu couldn't stop the flutter of her heart. Every brush of AJ's arm against hers, every subtle smile cast in her direction, summoned confusion. When they settled on their selection, AJ insisted on paying.

"I thought I invited you to breakfast?"

"You can pay me in another way." He met her eyes, then took a bite of his doughnut.

"Let me guess—in answers?"

"Is it so much to ask?" They stepped back outside together. "Blu, I think I've been pretty laid-back about everything. But, time is running out. I need some idea of what's on your mind."

Blu noticed the way his eyes creased and the dip of his voice. For the first time she recognized that she wasn't just a challenge for AJ. Her evasive behavior seemed to be hurting him.

"Okay, one question. Only one. And I promise, I'll

answer it truthfully."

"That's a lot of pressure."

"I think you can handle it." Blu leaned back against the side of her car and took a sip of her coffee.

"Fine." He stepped down from the curb in front of her. "But once I ask, I expect an actual answer. No jokes, no tricks."

"Okay." Blu set her coffee down on the top of the car.

CHAPTER 23

Blu looked up into AJ's eyes and tried to ignore the fact that his muscular frame was so close to her. Her heart slammed against her chest. "Ask away."

"What are you so afraid of?" His gaze lingered on hers.

Blu willed herself not to look away from him. "I'm not afraid."

"You promised to tell the truth." He raised an eyebrow.

Blu took a deep breath and released it slowly enough to buy her some time. When she reached the end of her exhalation, he still stood there, waiting.

"I guess I'm afraid of the impossibility of it all. I mean, summer is over. We're not going to keep in touch. What if I'm hired by a new family in a different state or with different demands on my time? What's the point of starting something that is only going to end?" She cleared her throat to cover the waver in her voice. "It wouldn't be fair to either of us to go through something like that.

Would it?"

"All of that is perfectly logical—if you think that anything could keep me away from you. The only impossibility, to me, is watching you walk away without ever giving me the chance to prove to you how much I care." He reached out and brushed her hair back over her shoulder. His fingertips glided along the rise of her shoulder and lightly along the slope of her upper back.

Blu shivered at his touch and tried to focus on his words as he continued.

"The only thing I'm afraid of is living the rest of my life without ever giving this a chance. Doesn't that terrify you, Blu? I don't believe that you don't feel it too—this thing between us. It's been building all summer. And to be honest with you, I've been waiting for it to fade. I told myself that it wasn't anything more than infatuation. But I was wrong. Because every single time I see you, it feels stronger." He took a slight step back and looked at her intently. "I don't think it will ever stop."

Blu couldn't resist a smile at his words. They were everything she'd hoped to hear, and at the same time, everything she'd been afraid of.

"AJ, all of the beautiful intentions aren't going to stop the summer from coming to an end."

He sighed and looked up at the sky for a moment. When he looked back at her she could see a faint glow in his eyes, as if he'd captured a bit of the sun.

"We're more than the summer, Blu." He locked his

eyes to hers as he rested his hands against the roof of the car on either side of her.

She watched his chin dip and his lips part to draw a breath in. Her heart raced in anticipation for the kiss. She knew all she had to do was turn her head and he'd catch her cheek instead, but she was frozen by her desire to believe every word that he'd just said to her.

Just as their lips were as close as they could be without actually touching, the sound of a police siren made them both jump. The only thing that touched was their foreheads, and not lightly.

AJ straightened up while Blu rubbed her palm across her forehead.

Chief Pitman stared out the window of his patrol car at them. "Why did I get a report of two people who match your description entering a residence without permission?"

AJ reached up and ran his hand back through his hair. "I have no idea."

"Who called it in?" Blu crossed her arms.

"I've had a car sitting at Betty's house ever since I picked up Wayne to question him."

"It might have been a good idea to tell me that, Uncle Paul."

"I had no reason to believe that you would invade someone's home. Did I?" He frowned. "Listen, Blu, I trust your instincts, and I appreciate your insight into the case, but you have taken things a little too far here. You could have, and should have, both been arrested for that stunt." He paused a moment and stared from one to the other before he continued. "Luckily for you, the patrol officer contacted me to find out what I wanted him to do."

"Thank you, Chief Pitman." Blu flushed at the thought of being brought home to Rachel and Marshall in a police car. She wouldn't have her job very long after that.

"Yes, thank you, but it would have been better if you'd told me in the first place," said AJ.

"It might have been better if you'd let me in on the little plan that you two hatched, hm?" Chief Pitman stared at his nephew. "I don't want to be left out of the loop about anything from now on. Understand?"

"Yes, sir." Blu nodded. "We did find something that you might think is interesting."

"What's that?"

Blu pulled up the picture of the banner on her phone. "It matches the inscription on the ring."

"That it does." Chief Pitman stroked his hand down along his jaw and chin. "I think you might be on to something here. We still haven't been able to pinpoint who the ring belongs to, but this banner might point us in the right direction. I'll have the techs check it out, or should I just forward it to Maddie?" He tilted his head in Blu's direction.

Blu's eyes widened at his words. "You know about

that?"

"There's not much that happens in this town without my knowledge. I do have to say that Maddie is good at what she does, and any friend of yours is someone that I'm fairly certain I can trust."

"I appreciate that. I'll let her know that you're a fan."

"Blu, I just don't know how I'm going to solve crime when you leave town." Chief Pitman grinned. "It certainly won't be as much fun."

"Don't worry, there's a good chance I'll be back next summer—in case you want to save all of the crime-solving for then." Blu grinned.

"Something tells me that you won't be able to wait that long. I don't know why, but I have a feeling that I'm going to be hearing from you before winter even sets in."

"I'm not sure. I may need to hang up my detective hat. I owe Maddie a lot of homework help."

"Ugh, homework." AJ shook his head. "You couldn't pay me enough."

"Maybe if you'd gone to the tutoring sessions that I set up for you in high school—"

"Uncle Paul." AJ narrowed his eyes.

"Right, right—all grown up. I get it." He laughed. "You two enjoy the clambake tonight. I'll be over there later to check in. Just be careful. The moment that you get involved in something like this, you take a risk. Stick together." He winked at Blu.

"I won't let her out of my sight." AJ wrapped his arm

around her shoulders.

Blu shrugged his arm off.

"I think he's telling me to look out for you, AJ." Blu smirked.

"You two fight that out, I've got work to do." Chief Pitman got back into his car and flashed the lights as he drove off.

CHAPTER 24

"Uncle Paul was talking about me looking out for you. You know that, right?" AJ raised an eyebrow.

"I don't know. I'm pretty tough," said Blu.

"You think so?" He crossed his arms. "You don't need a big burly man to protect you, hm?"

"Nope. Not one bit." Blu set her jaw.

"Let's just see about that." AJ moved so fast that Blu let out a shriek of surprise as he scooped her right up off of the ground and into his arms. "Hm. You might need me to put you down, huh?"

"You'll put me down if you know what's good for you." Blu wriggled in his grasp.

"I don't know. This is rather enjoyable." He tightened his grip. "You can't get away from me now, can you?" He met her eyes.

Blu stared back into his arrogant smile. Suddenly she didn't feel the need to fight.

He laughed and set her down on her feet. "It's not so bad having me around, see?"

"Not so bad. But if you keep trying to prove what a big burly man you are, we're going to miss the clambake."

"Well, we can't have that." He grabbed her hand and pulled her toward the car.

Blu laughed as he opened the door for her with a deep bow.

"You're right, I could get used to this."

"I think you should." He winked at her and walked around to the other side of the car.

As they drove to the clambake, Blu couldn't help looking over at AJ. The more she thought about not seeing him again, the more her chest ached. He was more than just a romantic interest. He had become a close friend and a partner in her investigations. Was it right of her to even consider cutting off contact just because she had feelings for him too?

The two fell into a tense silence as she wondered if his thoughts wandered in the same direction.

Blu parked the car and stared at the crowd that filled the entrance of the clambake. "Busy."

"Very." AJ looked out through the windshield but didn't make a move to get out.

"Ready to go in?"

He glanced over at her. "I'm not sure."

"What's wrong?"

"It's just that I've been looking forward to spending the day with you—without all the talk of the investigation, I mean. I feel like if we go in there, we're just going to be investigating. I wanted our day to be special. Is that selfish of me?" He looked over at her.

"No, I don't think so." She smiled. "I'm sorry. I've been caught up in this case, and you're right. We agreed to spend the day together. So, I'll do my best to keep my mind off the case. It's in your uncle's hands now."

"Promise?"

"Promise." Blu opened her door.

AJ followed suit. He met her at the front of the car and slid his arm around her waist. A large archway was erected above the beach access ramp. Local kids had decorated it with ribbons, lights, and plenty of glitter. Blu took the time to appreciate it.

"I bet Marley loves this."

"They did a great job." AJ held out his hand to her.

Blu didn't hesitate to take it. When they stepped through the archway, they were greeted by the delicious scent of the clambake already in progress. There were also many other food vendors set up along the beach.

In the distance, Blu could see a bounce house and game area set up for the kids. She could hear live music close by. Some people were dancing, others splashed in the water not far off. As packed as the beach was, it seemed that the entire community had come out for the clambake.

"Do you go to this every year?" Blu glanced at AJ.

"Just about. One year I was sick. Another year, we were away. Other than that, we've been here, taking part in all this. Sometimes it's hard for me to believe that we could have grown up so differently. I spent my time surfing and you've spent yours curled up on a bale of hay."

"Maybe, but we both had one thing in common," said Blu.

"What's that?"

"People who loved us." She smiled at him. "And that's what's most important, huh?"

"You're right about that. My uncle might be difficult, but he always took care of us. My mother died when I was young, and my father wasn't capable of raising us. So we ended up in the care of a single man who'd never even imagined having kids. Trust me, it was a bit of an adjustment for all of us, but most of all for him." AJ shook his head. "I get that now, but boy, did I give him hell as a teenager."

"I'm sorry. That must have been very difficult for you."

"Not as difficult as it could have been. Uncle Paul had the option to turn us over to the system, but he didn't. That's one of the things I admire about you too, Blu. I see the way that you love those kids, even though they're not even related to you. You get what it's like to love someone, because of who they are, not because of who they are to you."

"Yes, I guess I do." She smiled. "I really enjoy being part of their lives while I am. Even though I move on when I go to a new family, I always think about the kids."

"What happens when you move on? I mean, do you end up in different places?"

"Well, usually it happens when the kids get older— often around maybe middle school or high school. They're more independent, so the parents don't need as much help. Then I get a chance to start all over again. And yes, sometimes it's in different places."

"Do you think you'll ever want to settle down in one place?"

"Yes, I think I will. When I'm ready."

AJ looked toward the sound of a ringing bell and grinned. "Oh, this is something that we have to have."

"What?" Blu looked in the direction that he was pointing. "Oh, cotton candy?" She grinned. "It's been so long since I've had that. Sometimes I will get it for the kids, but never for me."

"Why not?" He tugged at her hand. "This is supposed to be fun, remember?"

"Nothing says fun like pink sugar." Blu laughed.

"I'll get us some. Wait here." He hurried toward the vendor.

CHAPTER 25

Blu couldn't help but smile at how excited AJ seemed. She breathed a sigh of relief as she realized he was right. They needed a few hours to just enjoy one another. The more she got to know AJ, the more certain she was that she wanted him to continue to be a part of her life.

She saw him walking toward her again with a large fluff of blue in one hand.

"Want a bite?" He held out the cotton candy to her.

Blu smiled as she looked into his eyes. "Yes, I think I do." She leaned forward.

"You got some on your nose." He laughed and reached out to wipe it away. Instead of touching the tip of her nose, his fingertips brushed along the curve of her lips. "Sorry."

"Why don't we take a walk along the water?" She wiped the cotton candy away.

"Sure." They walked hand in hand down to the water.

Blu took another bite of the cotton candy as they made their way along the beach.

"So, do you think we should talk about what we're

both trying not to talk about?" AJ gave her hand a light squeeze.

Blu tensed. She'd known this moment was coming, and she wanted to put it off a little longer, but she was out of excuses and she knew that AJ wasn't going to just let it drop.

"I guess we should." She paused a few feet away from some of the buildings that lined the old beach parking lot. When she looked at AJ, his expression looked somber.

"I think the fact that you look like you're about to go in front of a firing squad tells me everything that I need to know."

"AJ, that's not true."

"Look, I'm not trying to force you into anything, Blu." He paused and looked out over the water. "Okay, maybe I am. I mean, I know what I want, and I've been hoping that you want the same thing. But it's becoming clear to me that it's not the case."

"AJ, you have to give me a chance to talk." Blu reached for his hand but froze when she heard a scream.

The scream was cut off before it died out, as if someone had silenced the person. Her heart raced as she looked around. AJ looked as if he'd been startled as well. With all the noise of the clambake it was hard to pinpoint the direction that it had come from.

"We have to find out where she is." Blu started to walk around the side of one of the buildings.

AJ grabbed her by the elbow and pulled her back.

"Slow down. Wherever that scream came from, we need to be careful. We don't know what we could be walking into."

"We have to get to whoever it is. Fast, AJ!" Blu pulled away from him and hurried around the side of the building.

AJ dropped his cotton candy and quickly caught up with her. Together they crept along another small storage building. Blu could hear the faint sound of shoes scuffing across concrete. When she peered past a grouping of trees into a small dimly lit parking lot, she saw James Carry. His shoulders were hunched as he leaned forward. His hands were wrapped around a woman's throat—not just any woman—Blu was sure it was Cathy.

Blu surged forward without a second thought. "Hey! Stop that! Let her go!"

James looked sharply in her direction but did not let Cathy go.

AJ brushed past Blu and grabbed James by the shoulders. He tried to pull the man back away from Cathy.

James let go of Cathy, but as he turned to face AJ, he pulled a gun from his waistband.

Cathy slumped to the ground. Blu rushed to her side to check to make sure that she was okay. When she felt the woman's pulse it was strong. Cathy opened her eyes and looked up at her with gratitude.

CHAPTER 26

"Don't do it, James. Don't."

Blu looked back toward AJ's voice to see that he had his hands raised in the air.

James was pointing the gun at him as he looked over at Blu and Cathy.

"Any of you make a sound and I drop him, understand?"

Blu's eyes widened with fear. She never imagined that AJ would be put in danger by all this.

Cathy clung tightly to her arm as Blu tried to stand up. "Don't! He's crazy."

"Shut up!" James barked his command at Cathy.

Blu could feel her tremble next to her in reaction to the force of his voice.

"Cathy, just try to be calm." Blu whispered her words as she met the woman's eyes, but Cathy looked away fast. Blu didn't move a muscle. She knew that AJ's life was at stake.

"This isn't you, James. This isn't you at all. Put down the gun and we'll figure all this out." Blu tried to keep her voice calm, but inside she was petrified.

"You have no idea who I am—or what I'm capable of. Don't think to question me."

"James, this is Cathy—a waitress—she never did anything to you. Why not just let her go?"

"Oh, she did something alright, and she's not going anywhere."

"What is it? What did she do?"

"Please stop." Cathy shook her head and blinked back tears. "You two don't understand. He's not going to let any of us go. I do know who he is—what he's capable of."

"And whose fault is that?" James shouted. "Who decided to stick their nose in where it didn't belong?"

"James, stop!" AJ took a slight step forward. "You're out of control. What could she have possibly done to you?"

"Back off!" He pointed the gun at AJ.

AJ froze once more.

"Don't even think about it, James! I promise you, if you hurt him, you'll pay with more than your freedom." Blu started to move toward the pair.

Cathy's high-pitched voice stopped her. "Please! Please stop! It's all my fault. It really is. Because the truth is, I saw what he did. I saw him throw George down in the mud and hold him down. Then I saw him flip the boat over on top of him. I kept waiting for George to crawl out, but he didn't."

"I saw her looking out through the window." James glared at Cathy. "I knew then that if she told the police, there was going to be a problem. I was in such a hurry to wash my hands of the mud, I guess my ring slipped off in the process. I went up to the cafe and I warned her not to say anything. I made her promise that she wouldn't. Then I find out that she's been talking to you two, and imagine my surprise when she gets a visit from Chief Pitman." He scowled in AJ's direction. "I imagine that you had something to do with that."

"My uncle was investigating a crime. That doesn't mean that Cathy turned on you. In fact, all she told us was that she'd seen Xavier. We weren't even sure that it was you, until the moment that I saw you attacking Cathy. So your own actions are what caused all these problems."

"All I wanted to do was help protect my neighborhood. That's all. No one else would take a stand against these disgusting criminals. Instead, we've all been faced with nothing but increased crime.

"I went to George. I tried to get him help—to give him options other than a life of crime. He ignored my requests. I went to him again and warned him that if he continued to operate his little drug smuggling game, I'd make sure that he was taken out. He continued. So I made sure that a sting was set up to catch him in the act. But no matter how hard they tried they couldn't figure out where he was stashing the drugs. So I pulled the surveillance.

"I was just going to talk to George again. I wanted to see if he'd be willing to take a plea deal and work against his partner. When he saw me, he got angry, I got angry—one thing led to another and eventually I had to pin him down. Once I realized he couldn't breathe—well—" James paused and tightened his grip on the gun. "I've never killed anyone before, but I just thought to myself, all I have to do to end this is keep him pinned down. It felt like the right thing to do. Even after he stopped fighting, I didn't regret it. It felt like after all my years of trying to make a difference, I'd finally made an actual difference. He was a miserable man who was invading a good town. How could I let that happen?"

"Maybe you were right." Blu stepped forward just an inch or two.

James locked eyes with her as she continued speaking. "Maybe the only way to get rid of scum like George is for a good man to take a stand and do what you did. The only problem is, that's not what you're doing now. Is it?" Blu narrowed her eyes. "Now you're trying to kill an innocent woman. You're holding the police chief's nephew hostage, along with a nanny. How is that being the good guy? If you continue this, your one good act is going to be lost to the cruel and unjust actions that you're taking now."

"Blu, be careful." AJ curled his hands into fists.

CHAPTER 27

Blu could see from the tension of AJ's muscles that he probably wanted to step in front of her to shield her. But he knew better. The last thing that any of them needed to do was make a sudden move.

"It can't be helped. Can it?" James shook his head but continued to aim the gun at AJ. "There's nothing that can be done now. She knows too much. You all do."

"And a quadruple murder is not worse than running some drugs?" Blu looked at him with a slight shake of her head. "You know better than this, James. Right now, you've made a mistake. A jury will understand that you let your anger get out of control. Maybe they'll even buy that it was self-defense, if you tell them that George attacked you. But if this happens—if you kill all of us—no jury is going to let you get away."

"No one has to know it was me." James growled his words and flicked his eyes between all three of them. "If all the witnesses are gone."

"Please." Blu rolled her eyes and crossed her arms,

though she moved very slowly. "You're talking about murdering the chief of police's nephew, who he's raised as his own son. Do you think he's just going to let that go? Let's not forget that I work for some very wealthy people who are going to notice when their nanny doesn't come home. And don't you think it's possible that Cathy already told the police who she was protecting? Or maybe a friend or a coworker? Do you plan to kill everyone that she might have come in contact with?"

"Shut up. You don't know what you're talking about."

"Yes, she does." AJ drew James's attention back to him. "She knows that if you kill me, my uncle will never rest. He already knows that you're a suspect. You're not going to be able to get away with this. We found your ring."

"You did not. If you did, I'd already be in handcuffs."

"My uncle didn't believe that you could be involved. But I promise you, it won't take him long to figure out that ring was yours, that you were there, and that you are responsible for my death, along with the deaths of two innocent women. That is not going to look good to a judge. Think it through, James. If you pull that trigger, it's all over."

James was silent. Blu saw the tension in his features.

AJ must have sensed that James was ready to break, as he spoke up again. "Just put down the gun, James. This isn't you." AJ held his gaze and stretched out his hand to him. "This isn't the legacy that you want to leave behind.

You want to protect the community, not tear it apart with an incident like this. It's the clambake. It will never happen again, you know. No one will want to attend if there's a chance of crime happening. Just give me the gun and all this will be over."

"What's to stop you from shooting me?" James scowled. "Do you think I'm stupid?"

"He won't hurt you, James," Blu said. "He's not that kind of person. He doesn't want to cause any harm. He only wants to help. That's why he's here right now. He wants to help you out of this situation."

AJ's cell phone began to ring. He kept his hands in the air.

Blu guessed that it was Chief Pitman calling. He intended to meet them at the clambake, but how would he ever find them where they were? She had to do something to get Chief Pitman to realize that they were in danger.

While James was occupied with AJ, Blu slid her hand into her pocket. She found the button on her phone to turn it on. She had no way to figure out which number was which. So instead of trying to call Chief Pitman directly, she dialed 911. She left the line open in her pocket and hoped that James wouldn't notice any noise that came from it.

"Give me your phone."

Blu's heart dropped until she realized that James was speaking to AJ.

AJ moved his hand to his pocket and carefully withdrew his phone. He held it out to James.

When James reached for the phone, AJ lunged forward and grabbed the muzzle of the gun. The two men fought for a few seconds before James ripped the gun free of AJ's grasp.

Blu couldn't stop from screaming, as she was sure that James would fire it.

Instead, he grabbed Blu around the waist and pulled her in front of his body. He pointed the gun at AJ.

"Stupid move. Now I know I can't trust you. So me and your girlfriend here are going to be on our way."

"You can't take her anywhere." AJ started to move forward but stopped himself when James pointed the gun at Blu. "Please, don't hurt her."

Blu looked into AJ's eyes for a long moment before James started to pull her away from the other two. She did her best to make her body as heavy as possible by relaxing her muscles. When James stumbled in reaction to the dead weight, she heard a shout from just behind her.

"Drop your weapon!"

Blu sensed James relinquishing his grip on her. She broke free and ran straight toward AJ. Behind her she was aware that James was being thrown to the ground.

AJ opened his arms to her and pulled her close. He held on to her as her body shook. "It's over, Blu. It's okay. It's over."

Blu turned her head to look back and saw Chief

Pitman drag James to his feet.

"You're under arrest for murder, and I'm sure I'll come up with a few other things as well." Chief Pitman jerked James's hands behind his back.

"You should understand more than anyone, Chief! George deserved to die! He was ruining our town."

"Oh, maybe—maybe you had a chance at a deal or some mercy if you would have come forward right away. Maybe you could have pleaded insanity for thinking you had the right to decide who deserved to die. But you messed with my family, my town, and my best nanny detective. So now I'm going to make sure that you face the consequences for your crimes. Maybe our town isn't perfect, but it's full of people who care enough to know the difference between right and wrong. You are not one of those people."

James struggled as Chief Pitman pulled him away, but the moment the chief led him into the crowd of people he straightened up and walked with pride.

CHAPTER 28

Blu shook her head. "It's all about the show with him. He just wants to look good."

She was comfortable in AJ's arms. For the first time, she didn't try to pull away from him. In fact, she hoped that he wouldn't let her go any time soon.

AJ kissed her on her forehead. "He's not going to look great in an orange jumpsuit. Are you okay?"

"I am, if you are." She peeked up at him.

"I am." He held her gaze. "I don't know how my uncle knew to be here, but he saved us."

"If you hadn't talked James down the way you did, he would have ended this a while ago, AJ." Blu reached into her pocket and pulled out her phone, hanging up the line. "I dialed 911 and hoped that your uncle would somehow figure out what was happening. I guess that he did."

"When he couldn't reach me, he probably did a search for both our phones. The 911 call sends an alert up in the system. You're a genius, Blu. Who knows how this would have turned out if you hadn't thought so fast?"

"I don't know about that, but I'm glad we're safe."

"Thanks to the two of you." Cathy walked up to them with her hands shoved deep in her pockets. "If you hadn't shown up when you did, I'm sure I wouldn't be standing here right now. I'm sorry that I lied to you. I should have told you the truth from the beginning, then none of this would have happened."

"Maybe now you know that you can trust Chief Pitman." Blu glanced in the direction of the chief and James as they continued through the crowd toward the main parking lot.

Cathy stared after him as well. "I do. I wish I'd trusted him in the first place. After he came to talk to me last night, I was scared. James told me that if I went to the cops he'd know, and he'd come after me. He acted like he was such a hero, but he was nothing more than a criminal. I was going to leave town and just disappear. But I knew he'd be able to find me. So I sent him a message to meet me here. I thought in the crowded public place he wouldn't dare to hurt me. I just wanted to make it clear that I didn't tell Chief Pitman anything—that I never even let him in the door. But he wouldn't listen to me. He accused me of setting him up, and then he tried to kill me." She reached up and rubbed her bruised neck. "Even when it was happening, I kept waiting for him to let me go. I didn't believe I could have been so wrong about someone."

"The important thing is that you're safe." AJ smiled at her. "You really were dealing with a dangerous man."

"I was just afraid of the wrong one. I never thought that James would hurt me. He seemed like a superhero, you know?"

"The thing with superheroes is that they're not real. The only heroes that I've ever met wear badges and they know exactly how to protect a town without having to murder anyone."

"That's true." Cathy shook her head. "I guess it's finally over. I wonder if James will get off easy because of his political connections."

"He might." AJ cringed. "But I can guarantee you that my uncle will fight him every step of the way. A man like that needs to pay the price for what he's done. In his mind he took justice into his own hands, but in reality he just revealed himself to be what he's always been—a killer. I'm sure that my uncle is going to want your statement."

"I'll give it." Cathy rocked back on her heels. "I'll tell every single bit of it. Maybe George was a scumbag, but he didn't have to die the way he did. He didn't have to be treated that way."

"No, he didn't." Blu squeezed AJ's hand. "I'm glad that it's over. I'm ready to enjoy the rest of the clambake."

"Me too." AJ's voice was warm as he looked into her eyes.

As the two walked back toward the festivities, the adrenaline rush that Blu had experienced when James grabbed her finally began to subside. She continued to cling to AJ's hand, as if she was afraid that letting it go would make him disappear. Earlier, when she'd seen the gun pointed at him, she knew in that moment how it could feel to possibly lose him—how she'd feel if he weren't in her life.

Blu was feeling way too preoccupied with everything that they'd been through to enjoy any of the activities that they tried to participate in. Most of the people at the clambake had no idea what had been happening only a few feet away from them.

"Blu, you're not okay, are you?" AJ turned her toward him. "You look upset. Maybe I should take you home so you can rest."

"It's not that, AJ."

"No?" He brushed her hair back from her eyes. "Then what is it? Tell me, please."

"AJ, there's something I want to talk to you about." The moment she spoke the words she knew that there was no turning back. The murder was solved, but her personal life wasn't.

AJ's eyes shifted from wide open and questioning to narrowed. His lips twitched from a faint smile into a frown. "Here, let's get away from all the noise." He drew her away from the crowd and out toward the water.

CHAPTER 29

Once Blu and AJ were alone close to the edge of the water, she turned to face him, taking his hand in hers. "AJ, I'm sorry for the way I treated you all summer. You made it clear to me what you wanted, and I did my best to avoid it. That wasn't right."

He curled his hand around hers and held it tight even as he turned away from her. "Please don't."

"Don't what?" She took his other hand as well, which forced him to turn to face her.

"I know what you're going to say." He looked down at their fingers intertwined rather than into her eyes. "I'm not ready to hear it. I'm sorry. I know how you feel, and I'm trying to be okay with it, but I'm just not."

"What do you know, AJ?" Blu tightened her grasp on his hands. "I don't think you understand."

"No, I honestly don't. I don't think I ever will." He looked at her. "I don't want this to be goodbye. I don't know why it has to be. All summer you've evaded me— pushed me away. I thought, okay, she's just testing me.

She needs to see that I'm trustworthy. I think I've given you plenty of reason to trust me, but still, you seem so unsure. So I thought, maybe she's just not interested. Maybe some loser from the beach who barely owns a bar just isn't her type—"

The sudden presence of her lips pressing against his silenced him. She drew his hands around her waist and molded her body to his as he lurched into the kiss. Dizziness swirled through Blu's senses as every nerve in her body came alive with warmth. It was as if she could no longer feel the sand beneath her feet, or the weight of the sky above her. She was anchored only by the glide of his lips against hers.

She hung onto his neck as if she might be swallowed up by the earth if she let go. Her heart pounded so hard that she was sure it would burst, until she realized that it was his heart that she felt. What started out in a passionate frenzy slowed to a subtle savoring caress, so tender that her entire body relaxed.

When his lips left hers, every doubt, every hesitation, every logical reason to avoid him disappeared from Blu's mind and heart. It stunned her that this was what she'd been avoiding all summer.

In all of her experiences in life, she never imagined love to feel so good. She thought it was all chemicals and instincts. She never comprehended the level of connection that could occur between two people when they were both open to it.

"It doesn't have to be goodbye, Blu." He looked into her eyes, and for the first time she understood why she felt such recognition when she looked at him. It wasn't because of some chance meeting when they were kids. It was because he was the man she'd been comparing every other man to her entire life, without ever knowing it.

"No, it doesn't." She held his gaze. "I'm not going to say it, AJ. I promise. If you don't say it, I won't say it."

"Are you sure?" He searched her eyes. "Because I don't think I can survive a disappearing act."

"I'm not going anywhere." She smiled. Then her smile faltered. "Well, that's not exactly true. I am going to Manhattan. But apparently there's something called video chat?"

He laughed and wrapped his arms around her in a tight hug. "Oh, yes. And many other things. Thank you."

"For what?"

"For being you." He kissed her again, just as the sun began to spread its evening glow along the waves. Just when he turned back to her for another kiss, his cell phone rang. He laughed as he looked at the screen.

"My uncle has the worst timing. Excuse me a second."

Blu grinned as he answered the phone.

"Okay, thanks for the information. Yes, of course we'll fill out whatever is needed. Thanks, Uncle Paul." He hung up the phone and looked at Blu. "It turns out that it was James's ring on the beach. The banner we found in

Betty's house was from a college—the same college that James went to, and—surprise, surprise—George also went to."

"George went to college?"

"I guess he didn't do too well, but James and George were in the same fraternity. Maybe that's why James was so angry with George for what he was doing."

"I guess." Blu shook her head. "It's shocking that they could have ended up on two very different paths."

"Were they so different?" AJ shrugged. "One led to drug dealing, another led to murder."

"You're right, I guess they weren't." Blu rested her head against his shoulder. "I guess that just proves that we never know what the future holds."

"I know what I hope it holds."

"Me too." Blu smiled and met his lips for another kiss.

When news of the councilman's arrest broke that evening, the scandal spread fast.

Blu arrived back at the beach house to find Marshall and Rachel watching the latest news update.

"Oh, Blu, I'm so glad you're home." Rachel stood up when she saw her come in. "The reporter mentioned that the police chief's nephew was involved and I knew you were supposed to be with AJ today."

"I'm sorry I worried you." Blu frowned. "I didn't know they were saying that on the news."

"Are you hurt?" Marshall frowned. "Were you with him when it all happened?"

Blu bit into her bottom lip. She didn't want to lie to Rachel and Marshall, but she didn't want to worry them either.

"I'm safe now. I just hope that the councilman gets the justice that he deserves."

"That's not exactly an answer, is it?" Rachel glanced over at Marshall and then back at Blu.

"It's okay, Rachel. Blu's entitled to her mysteries. All that matters is that she's okay and ready to head back to Manhattan with us, right, Blu?"

"Absolutely." Blu smiled. "So, can I help you pack?"

CHAPTER 30

Over the next two days, Blu helped the family get ready to return to the city. She and the kids also spent quite a bit of time on the beach. Though she was busy, she noticed that she didn't hear too much from AJ. When she did, he mentioned that he was helping his uncle with the case and the media onslaught that it had caused.

On the morning of the drive back to Manhattan, Blu's stomach was in knots. She'd hoped that AJ would want to be part of her last day, but he hadn't mentioned meeting her that morning. She also hadn't had a text from him that morning to even say goodbye. She was tempted to text him herself, but she thought that might be bothersome.

Blu stood beside her car and flipped through her phone. She wanted to call AJ, but she didn't think she should. It would be hard to say goodbye, and he obviously hadn't made an attempt to contact her. She sighed as she put her phone back in her pocket.

Rachel waved from her car as she, Marshall, and the kids headed out of the driveway.

Blu waved back with a bright smile. Even if she wasn't feeling very positive, she didn't want the kids to know that. It was the first time she'd dreaded going back to Manhattan. Maybe that one kiss between them had been enough for AJ to realize that it wasn't worth all the trouble.

The problem was, that the one little kiss had seemed to have the opposite affect on Blu. It made her believe that he was worth any trouble she might face during a long-distance relationship. There was no way she could go back to thinking that she could live without him. It made her feel silly to wait next to her car in the hopes that he would call.

She pulled out her phone again—no text, no phone call. She frowned and opened the door to her car. She tossed her phone inside. With one last look in the direction of the beach house she decided it was time to leave it all behind. If AJ wanted to find her, he knew where she'd be. If not, then she had been right all along.

As she started to get into the car, she heard the roar of an engine. She looked up to see AJ's jeep block the base of the driveway. He hopped out of the jeep with a giant bouquet of flowers in his hand.

A wide smile spread across Blu's lips.

"You weren't trying to skip town on me, were you?" He grinned as he walked up to her. "Because you know my uncle's a cop, and he can hunt you down."

"I'm counting on it." Blu smiled back and leaned in

for a kiss. She pulled back and looked into AJ's eyes. "I didn't think you were coming."

"I wanted it to be a surprise."

"I'm surprised."

He wrapped his arms around her. "Just remember, this isn't goodbye. Okay?"

"I believe you." She sighed and hugged him in return. "I'm glad you came." She pulled away and looked toward the car. "I really do have to get on the road. I don't want to be too far behind. The kids will be cranky after the car ride, and Rachel and Marshall will be tired."

"I won't keep you long. I'm sorry I didn't get here earlier. My uncle needed some help getting some reporters off his lawn. This James Carry situation is a big scandal."

"I hope it dies down soon. I know how much your uncle hates attention."

"And people on his lawn." AJ laughed. He held out a CD case. "Here, this is for you. Something to listen to on your drive."

"Aw, how sweet. Thank you." She read over the assortment of songs. "Just what I like."

"Maddie might have helped me out a bit with that."

"Oh, did she?" Blu raised an eyebrow and smiled. "She is always up to something."

"Only because she cares." He grabbed her hand and held on to it as he smiled. "You'll call me when you get to Manhattan?"

"Yes, I will."

"Promise?" He raised an eyebrow.

"Yes, I promise. I'll call you as soon as I get there." Blu laughed. "I don't think you need to worry about that."

"I hope not. Because I know how to get to Manhattan, you know."

"Hm. I'm not sure that I believe that." Blu offered him a smile.

"It's true. I might get lost a few times, but I'll get there." He narrowed his eyes. "And I have no problem with driving. I'm looking forward to you giving me a tour around the city. Hm? You still owe me an official date."

"Absolutely." She smiled at the thought of showing him all her favorite places. Then she leaned close and kissed his cheek. "I can't say that this isn't hard, though. I've gotten rather used to you being the best part of my day."

"It's not goodbye." He looked into her eyes for a long moment, then kissed her forehead. "It's just the first part of our next adventure."

Blu grinned as she thought of the school shopping, homework, and elaborate parties that waited for her in Manhattan. There was never a shortage of drama or things to do. She hoped that would be enough to distract her from missing AJ. She doubted it, but she still hoped.

"I think you might be right about that. No matter what kind of adventure it is, I'm glad I get to share it with you."

"Me too." He looked into her eyes and reached up to brush a bit of her hair back behind her ear. "It doesn't matter how far you wander, Blu, now you're part of my life, my heart, and my future."

"Whatever that future might be." Blu hugged him.

As she looked over AJ's shoulder toward the road that awaited her, she knew that as strange and wild as the journey ahead might be, she had the feeling that she wouldn't be navigating it alone—something which suddenly sounded very appealing to her.

ALL TITLES BY MACI GRANT

http://Amazon.com/author/macigrant
*Check the author page for current list of titles

Summer in Diamond Bay

#1 Lifeguards and Liars
#2 Sandcastles and Secrets
#3 Ice Cream and Intrigue
#4 Hot Dogs and Homicide
#5 Clambakes and Chaos